Better Than Sexy

Sexy Series Book #3
Club TEN29

CARLY PHILLIPS

Cover Photo: Sara Eirew
Cover Design: @Steamy Designs
Editor: Amy Knupp, Blue Otter Editing
Developmental Editor: Dana with Danja Tales

* * *

Insta-love only happens in the movies.

Insta-lust? That she'd buy into.

Until she meets take-charge club owner Landon Bennett and falls head over heels at a glance.

When hot as sin Landon Bennet offers sexy songstress Vivienne Clark a summer residency at his popular Manhattan nightclub, it's the opportunity of a lifetime and she can't resist. Add in the man's obvious interest and seductive attention and life is perfect. Until she puts together the pieces of his past. Fate might have brought them together, but is the intimate relationship they've been building strong enough to overcome the the secret Vivi is hiding?

A complete stand-alone

Chapter One

"IT'S OVER." LANDON Bennett sat at the bar of his club surrounded by his partners and best friends, Jason Dare and Tanner Grayson, exhaustion and relief seeping into his pores.

When the judge's gavel came down confirming Victor Clark's guilty plea for numerous crimes, not the least of which had been calling in a bomb threat to Club TEN29, vandalism, assault and violating his parole, all three men, Landon, Tanner, and Jason had breathed a sigh of relief.

The bastard who'd killed Landon's twin brother in a hazing initiation gone wrong would be going away again for a long, fucking well-deserved time. He never should have gotten out of prison in the first place, but apparently the government placed a high value on Vic's snitching on his cellmate, who'd been a bigger dirtbag than Vic himself.

"To Levi, to the future, and to Club TEN29." Which had been named for the date Levi died. Jason, from his seat on a barstool, raised his glass and they all took a drink.

Nonalcoholic because despite the fact that they owned a nightclub, none of the guys had a taste for liquor since they'd experienced that horrific night with Levi during their freshman year in college.

Landon drank his sparkling water and let out a long groan. "Now we just have to get through sentencing."

"Vic's parole was revoked and he was originally in for manslaughter. Add all these charges including a federal one, and we won't have to worry about seeing his face for a good long time. Don't worry."

This from Tanner, the hotheaded one of the trio. But being with Scarlett, the woman he'd recently met at the club, had mellowed Tanner. Just like Jason's relationship with Faith had changed him and put an easier smile on his face. Landon was happy for his friends, even if he couldn't see himself settling down any time soon.

His last serious girlfriend had cheated on him. While Landon had been working nights, she'd been doing her own thing in the evenings. Her own thing being her ex. Landon had left work early and gone over to her place to surprise her … and found her ex's face between her thighs. She shouldn't have given him her key. Suffice to say, after the jaded life he'd lived thus far, trust didn't come easily, except for the guys ... and his immediate family.

"So I know you've been wanting to talk to us about the club," Tanner said. "What do you have in mind?"

Landon was grateful for the subject change. The three men, who'd met in college, ran Club TEN29 together and made decisions as a team. Levi's death had bonded them in a way nothing else could have. Today they had a solid partnership. Tanner dealt with everything inside the club, Landon handled entertainment, and Jason held the position of CEO, running the business end of things. However, they tossed out ideas, collaborated, and made decisions good for them all.

Landon had been thinking about his idea since the night of Jason's thirtieth birthday party a few months ago, but they'd been so tied up with the Vic bullshit that he'd tabled the conversation. Until now.

"Can we agree that the night we hosted Tangled Royal was a huge success?" The popular band that included Jason's brother-in-law, Grey Kingston, had reunited for a one-night gig in order to help bring back customers to Club TEN29 after Vic's bomb threat had scared them away.

Both Jason and Tanner nodded. "We've been on an upswing ever since," Tanner said.

Landon leaned against the glass and wood bar.

Carly Phillips

"What's the big thing now?" Before they could consider, let alone answer, he said, "Las Vegas residencies. Britney Spears and Celine Dion were a success, now Kelly Clarkson, Keith Urban, Jennifer Lopez, all bringing in people. So I was thinking, why not host a summer residency here, at Club TEN29?"

His friends looked at each other and Landon let them think, his own gaze going to the darkened stage they'd put in when Jason had the idea of opening the club to live acts in order to give the place a more Miami Beach vibe.

A grand piano sat in the corner, and just looking at it, Landon's fingers itched to play. But he hadn't indulged in music since his brother was killed. Both he and Levi had shared a talent few possessed. They could hear a snippet, a piece of music, and immediately replay it on the keys. Same with quite a few other instruments. Prodigies, their parents had called them. Landon's desire to play had died along with his twin.

"Interesting idea," Jason said, drawing Landon's attention from the painful past. "Who did you have in mind?"

"I didn't. I've been tossing ideas around in my head but nothing's felt right." Landon knew the feel of what he wanted, he just hadn't laid eyes on the right performer yet.

"Grey is in Florida. No way he's leaving his family

4

for a two-month gig," Jason said. "Avery would string him up by his balls and he's not fighting with a very pregnant woman." He chuckled at the thought. "And Lola"—Tangled Royal's lead singer – "enjoyed the one night, but again, she's in Miami and not leaving her husband." Rep Grissom was the Miami Thunder football team's wide receiver and they were based in Florida.

"Yeah, I didn't expect to get that kind of star power for the summer." Landon drummed his fingers on the glass. "Any other suggestions?"

For the next few minutes, they tossed around names. Big, small, rock, classic, pop, indie, but they couldn't agree on the first person to approach.

Jason snapped his fingers and pulled his phone from his pocket. "Faith watched one of the morning shows on television earlier today. On their Pop News segment, they featured this woman whose performance video went viral. Vivi something or other. You should check her out. Great pipes. I don't think she's going to stay unknown for long. Let me search…" He input something into his phone and muttered to himself as he obviously scrolled through videos.

"While he looks, I want to make sure we're on the same page," Landon said. "When I say residency, I mean we need to provide a place for the performer to stay while they're in the city, assuming they don't already live here, and depending on what we agree to pay per performance, there may be supplemental payment or things we need to give as well." He looked to Jason, who was still scrolling through his phone.

As the CEO, he might find holes in the plan Landon had missed. Tanner, too. They complemented each other's strengths and weaknesses.

"We could offer the upstairs apartment," Tanner suggested. "Saves an additional rental fee and we don't use it much anymore."

Landon shook his head. "You two very much attached guys don't," he muttered.

Tanner shot him a wry glance. "When was the last time you hooked up upstairs, or anywhere, Landon? It's the cheapest solution."

Frowning, he gave the point to his partner. "Fine." He ignored answering the question because he couldn't remember the last time he'd had a good fuck. Or any fuck, for that matter.

He'd been over the club women for a long time and resistant to anyone who had the word *serious* written all over them. It would take a special woman to get him to change his mind, but he didn't deny it was possible. Although his ex had royally screwed him over, his parents had an amazing relationship and had been happily married for the last thirty-two years. Even his equally jaded best friends had found their forever women. Landon just didn't know if she existed for him.

"You're in charge of entertainment," Jason finally said, glancing up from the phone screen. "I'm going to assume you've done your research."

"Damn straight. I've also got our lawyer working on a contract in case you both agree." He grinned, knowing he was ahead of them, but hell, he believed in his idea.

Tanner shook his head and laughed. "Fine. I'm in. Jase?"

The other man nodded. "I like it. Now as for who … I found the video. Look." Jason rose from his seat and walked over to where Landon stood behind the bar and placed his phone on the counter.

The three men crowded around and looked down at the small screen. Jason tapped and the video filled the entire display.

A gorgeous brunette with long hair hanging down her back in sexy waves rocked her way across the stage. Despite the ball cap on her head, she had presence, owning the space as she moved, hips swaying, her husky voice crooning magic.

Landon leaned in, wanting to get closer to her, to view her as clearly as possible.

"Hey, back up so we can see," Tanner complained, smacking him in the arm.

Feeling oddly proprietary over the video, Landon reluctantly lifted his head and stepped to the side so his friends could also check out the spectacular woman on the screen. But she'd taken off her cap for a brief second, and his gaze was locked on her face, his body captivated by her voice, and his dick completely engaged in a way he hadn't been in years.

"I want her," Landon said, hoping his friends didn't realize he meant it in a wholly different way than as their summer resident performer.

"That's her," Tanner agreed, and a rush of adrenaline buzzed through Landon's veins.

"Then it's unanimous." Jason picked up his phone, taking away Landon's eye candy.

"Email me the video." Landon ran a hand over the back of his neck. "Also include anything you know about her so I can track her down and make the offer when we're ready."

Jason tapped on his phone. "Done," he said, and Landon's phone buzzed in his pocket. Something told him he'd be watching that video on repeat later tonight with his hand wrapped around his cock.

"Make sure the contract is in order before you jump the gun and go see her," Jason said. "I want to cover our asses and not get ourselves tied up with something we come to regret."

Landon nodded. "I'll call Ryan and set up a conference call after he emails the documents," he said of their attorney on retainer, Ryan Walker. "We'll all be in agreement before we go forward," Landon promised, his phone with the video burning a hole in his pocket.

He needed to see her again. To pause on her face, listen to her sing, and know whether or not the initial gut reaction that had his pulse thudding, his heart pounding, and his dick hard as hell had been real.

Because one look at the sexy songstress and Landon was hooked.

THE SOUND OF banging woke Vivienne Zane from a deep sleep. Exhaustion still nagging at her from her late night of tossing and turning, she dragged herself out of bed, pulled on a pair of pajama pants and a sweatshirt, and padded toward the door of her apartment.

She looked into the peephole and saw her best friend and personal assistant, Ellie Roberts, standing at the door, waving at her. "Let me in, sleepyhead! I have news!"

Vivi groaned and opened the door. "You'd better have coffee this early."

Ellie, with full makeup, blonde hair curling around her face, met her with a smile. "It's noon. And you won't need caffeine after you hear what I have to tell you." She pulled out her phone. "You went viral! I know you didn't want anyone to know you went out to sing, but oh my God, look at the views!"

Ellie shoved the screen in her face, and Vivi blinked in shock at the number of views beneath the video of her belting out her favorite tune.

"Vivi, this could lead to big things!"

And Lord knew they needed something to shake loose. Between bills that needed paying, her band that required money or they'd have to go their separate ways, and her family that had fallen apart thanks to her brother having been found guilty *again*, this time of so many crimes she'd lost count, she'd been emotionally drained for too long.

Needing a break, she'd just wanted to just be herself, not someone who had people counting on her to come through. She just wanted to be Vivi, the girl who got lost in music when life was hard. So one night last week, she'd put on a pair of worn jeans, an old tee shirt, and a baseball cap and made her way to a bar owned by an old friend, where she sang her heart out to drunk people.

"I didn't notice anyone with their phones on me." Then again, she hadn't been looking.

"Well, the contact email from your website has so many hits I'm never going to get through them all!" Ellie's excitement was tangible. "Oh my God! *Good*

Morning World picked it up on their Sunday Pop News segment!" She was practically bouncing on her heels, her body vibrating with contagious energy. "They used your actual music name!"

Vivi swallowed hard. She wasn't well known in the industry, but she was an up-and-coming artist known as Vivi Z, doing small gigs with her band and hoping to get a break.

"Let me look at it again," she said, now wide awake and realizing the implications of Ellie's news.

Her goals, to be a big-name pop star and to take care of her band and her people, were possibly within reach if they leveraged this opportunity the right way.

Ellie handed her the phone, and she began scrolling through the comments. To her shock, not only had the video gone viral, but her fans, people who'd found her as an up-and-coming indie artist, had recognized her and were clamoring for the song to be recorded.

"I'll be right back." She darted into the bedroom for her own phone, yanked it off the charger, and returned to her friend, already pulling up her social media pages, which were blowing up like crazy.

She looked up at Ellie in shock. "This is unreal."

Her friend grinned. "If the world didn't know who Vivi Z was before, they will now!"

Hard banging on the door sounded.

"Owen," they both said at the same time. Her

11

manager, Owen Rhimes, who had taken her on last year, would jump on this in a heartbeat.

Vivi strode to the entryway, glanced through the peephole, and nodded at Ellie before opening the door. "Owen, what a surprise," she said somewhat drolly.

He walked in, tablet in hand, wearing a pair of light-colored chinos and a green Polo tee shirt, collar up, as usual. "If I'd known you were doing anonymous gigs for no money, I'd have been pissed, Vivienne," he said, using her full name, as he always did. "However, given the outcome, I have no complaints. Now I just need to organize the offers that have already started coming in and present you with the best of the best." He sounded certain ... and full of himself, as if he'd had something to do with her big break.

She rolled her eyes at Ellie, behind his back, of course. He was such a pompous ass, but she'd needed an agent, and very few had been willing to take a risk on an unknown musician.

"I want to see all the offers." She never wanted to be an artist who blindly trusted her agent. She intended to be in charge of her own destiny.

He cleared his throat and frowned at her. "I know what's best, Vivienne."

"And it's my future. So I want to hear them all."

He glanced at his tablet. "Well, most involve tour-

ing as an opening act. The main acts aren't huge ...
yet, but I can make some calls and—"

"No touring, Owen. I want to be in one place so I
can hole up in a recording studio during the day and
work on new music. I want the time and money to
record."

"Beggars can't be choosers. We're lucky that these
offers are coming in, but there is no guarantee they'll
be around forever," he said, his tone full of impa-
tience.

He might have a point. Not that he wasn't a jerk at
times, but she needed to hear him out. "Let's sit down
and you can tell me what you've got so far."

For the next thirty minutes, he went through a list
of opportunities that included opening for B-list
bands, and if she wasn't so set on staying around the
northeast, both for recording and especially for her
mother, who was hurting from her brother's actions,
she might have jumped at the opportunity. But she'd
rather play local clubs for the year than take off on her
mother at such a difficult time for both of them.

Her father, Victor Clark Senior, had passed away
from a heart attack years ago, and that was both a
blessing and a curse, because he'd been a big contribu-
tor to the bully and abuser her brother, Vic, had
become, and Vivi carried her own share of guilt
because she'd been his baby girl, his princess. Her

brother had been his punching bag. But she preferred not to dwell on either of them now.

She refocused on her agent. "I'll think about all these, I promise. In the meantime, if something more local comes up, call me immediately." She really wanted a well-paying gig that would help her afford in-studio recording sessions.

She refused to take help from her mother, who ran a small legal practice but specialized in pro-bono work, so she didn't make much on her own.

Owen frowned and tapped on his watch. "Tick-tock. These offers aren't going to be open forever. I'll email you a summary of each."

She merely smiled at him. He ought to know she couldn't make a spur-of-the-moment decision. He rose and headed for the foyer. She ushered him out and closed the door behind him, leaning back against it with a sigh.

"He's such a killjoy," Ellie muttered.

"Yes. But he's my killjoy. The only one who'd take me on when no one else would. Now, for the love of God, can we please go get some coffee?"

THE NEXT DAY, Vivi and Ellie went to the gym, where Vivi did her daily run on the treadmill. Headphones on, she was lost in the beat of the music, when an alert from Owen came up on her phone. Since she'd done her requisite miles, she slowed down and came to a stop, checking her screen as soon as she'd caught her breath.

Call me now.

She pulled up his contact name and placed the call. He answered immediately. "Where've you been? Never mind. I need you in my office as soon as possible. I have a man sitting here with an offer that's going to blow your mind. It's everything you wanted."

She glanced down at her gym outfit, knew she was a sweaty mess, and groaned. "But—"

"No buts. I'm keeping him busy talking. Get down here," he barked.

"Owen! I'm in the gym. I need to go home and change!"

"No time. Hurry." He disconnected the call.

"Jesus. High-strung much?" she asked the empty air.

"What's wrong?" Ellie had climbed off her treadmill and was wiping down her face.

Vivi grabbed her own towel and began to wipe down, too. "Owen summoned me. He said he's got someone in his office I need to meet. *Now.* On the one hand, I can't go dressed like this. On the other hand, if I go home to shower and change, it's going to take me at least an hour."

She lived in a tiny apartment in Jersey City. Her gym wasn't close to her apartment. She chose both for their cheap cost and sucked up the hassle. But Owen's office was close to the gym, and she could be there within ten minutes once she got on the subway.

"Well, you've got deodorant in your bag and a little makeup. You're in leggings and a cropped top. If he's going to insist, it is what it is." Ellie walked alongside her as they headed for the locker room.

"I can't shower here and put these clothes back on. Gag. So you're right. A little powder and freshening up and it's as good as it's going to get." She pushed open the door and they walked into the women's locker area.

"Want me to join you?" Ellie asked.

Vivi nodded. "A second set of ears is always good. I might miss something."

They pulled themselves together as best they could. Thanks to the items the gym set out on the counters, Vivi used dry shampoo in her hair and piled it up into a messy bun and spritzed vanilla body spray on her when she finished washing, touched up her makeup, and called it a day.

A little while later, she and Ellie walked into Owen's office. Anya, his secretary, greeted them with a smile. "Hello, ladies. He's expecting you. Go on in."

Vivi knocked once and opened the door, letting

16

them inside.

Her agent remained seated but another man rose from his chair, and Vivi couldn't take her eyes off him. Tall, broad shouldered, with sexy scruff covering his face and incredibly blue eyes, he was, in a word, gorgeous. His hair was a dark brown, the front dipping lower on his forehead. And that full mouth was made for sin.

"Vivienne, did you hear me? This is Landon Bennett," Owen said.

She'd been caught staring, and a knowing grin lifted the other man's sensual lips. Because his eyes had raked over her spandex-clad body and said body had reacted in a very obvious way, she didn't feel bad. It would have been even more awkward if she wrapped her arms around herself and covered her now perky nipples, so she somehow kept them at her sides.

"A pleasure to meet you, Ms. Zane," he said.

"Hello, Mr. Bennett." Her voice sounded huskier than normal.

"Call me Landon." He stepped forward, extending his hand.

"I'm Vivi." She clasped her hand in his larger one, and a jolt of awareness licked through her veins.

Was it her imagination or did he hold on a second or two longer than was necessary? For sure when he released her, she felt the loss.

Ellie nudged her in the side and Vivi coughed. This man seriously had her off-kilter. "This is Ellie Roberts, my personal assistant."

"Nice to meet you, Ellie."

Even his voice was smooth and perfect, Vivi thought, and when he smiled at Ellie, as ridiculous as it sounded, Vivi was jealous he'd turned that megawatt grin on someone else.

"I'm sorry to have dragged you away from your workout." His gaze once again slid over her body, this time in a much more blatant appraisal.

Owen cleared his throat. "Now that the formalities are finished, we can move on to business," Owen suggested in his not-so-subtle way.

"Ladies?" Landon gestured toward the two open chairs, and they settled into their seats. Only then did he follow.

The man had more manners than her agent, she thought.

"So Vivienne, Landon owns Club TEN29 in Tribeca. I'm sure you've heard of it." Owen picked up his pen and tapped it against the desk.

She nodded. "You just had the live reunion concert for Tangled Royal." She'd read it in the trade blogs and sites online.

"That's right. We saw your viral video and we'd like to offer you a summer residency."

She blinked, certain she had to be hearing him wrong. "Residency?"

"Yes. Your agent has the contract." He tipped his head toward Owen, who had dollar signs in his eyes and was practically drooling on his desk.

Her heart squeezed in excitement; however, she heard her lawyer mother's voice inside her head. *Never show your hand, Vivi. Always say you'll think about it, then take the time to go over the contract. Show it to me. Don't rush in your excitement to grab a deal.* Her mother, Anne Marie Zane, who'd always believed in her.

"I appreciate the offer, Mr. ... I mean Landon," she said, doing her best to remain calm when all she wanted to do was scream, *I'll take it!*

"As I told you before Vivienne arrived, we have certain requirements," Owen said.

They did?

"Vivienne requires an upscale place to stay, food and beverage comped, and a rider with her list of particular items she will need on hand."

Ellie gasped, then covered it with a cough.

"Owen, these are all things we need to discuss first." She had an apartment in Manhattan. True, it was a month-to-month shithole, and she lived on tap water and whatever was on sale at the local grocery or bodega. She couldn't believe Owen was discussing her contract as if she were *somebody*.

19

Of course, that was what she paid him for, but she didn't want Landon to think she was a spoiled celebrity out to milk him for all he was worth. The things she wanted from this contract weren't frivolous or meant to make her look like a diva. They would help establish her future and pay off any debt she had now. But she'd get into her needs when it came to dealing with her agent. Negotiating with the man was Owen's job. She just didn't want him to make her look like a diva.

Landon's approving gaze flickered to her before he said, "Mark up the contract and forward it to my lawyer. Everything is up for negotiation and discussion. We want Ms. Zane to be happy." He turned his attention to her, definite interest in his gaze.

Her stomach warmed at the obvious attraction between them, which was definitely reciprocated. She didn't think it was a good idea to want the man who would be in charge of her employment, but she couldn't deny the desire she felt just looking at this powerful man with the handsome face and bedroom eyes.

"I wanted to present the offer in person because the summer residency idea is that important to me and my partners." He rose to his feet. "But please go over everything in detail and get back to me as soon as possible."

He walked over to her and extended his hand. She

slid her palm against his roughened one, and he pulled her to her feet. "It was nice to meet you and I look forward to you answer, Vivi. We could have an incredible summer together."

She swallowed hard, lost in the husky sound of his voice and the inherent promise in his words. "I'll go over the contract in detail and get back to you."

"Sounds like a plan." He glanced at Owen. "Thank you for your time." With another long glance at Vivi that had her heart pounding inside her chest, he strode out of the office. And she had to say, his backside was as spectacular as the front.

"Vivienne! You could have shown a little more excitement! This offer is exactly what you wanted."

Her heart pounded inside her chest and she turned to Ellie. "Oh my God! A residency! Can you believe this?" She flung herself at her friend and they hugged in excitement. Then she spun to face Owen. "I don't care about a place to live or specific food. I want them to pay me enough money for a recording studio during the day. I want to be able to move out of my shitty apartment, yes, but I'm more concerned about looking forward with my career."

"What if I could get you both?" He raised his eyebrows, certain in his abilities.

"Send me the contract, Owen. I'll go over it and send to my lawyer."

He narrowed his gaze. "I assure you I'm capable of handling the legal end as well. I'm an attorney, as you know."

She smiled, doing her best not to patronize him when all she was doing was looking out for herself. "It's good business to have a second look."

She tipped her head toward the door, and together, she and Ellie headed out.

"Oh my God. Did that really happen?" she asked her best friend.

Ellie grinned. "It did. If the contract is good, you've hit the jackpot. And what was that chemistry I noticed between you and Landon Bennett?" She waved her hand in front of her face.

"He's so sexy. I thought I was hit by a freight train when I looked into his eyes." She squeezed her thighs together and felt the rush of desire flood through her. The man had had a potent effect on her.

Ellie grinned. "Looks like it is going to be a long, hot summer."

Vivi certainly hoped so.

Chapter Two

BACK IN HER apartment, Vivi propped her feet on the chipped wooden table in front of her couch and opened her secondhand laptop. Although it'd been a couple of hours since she'd met with Landon Bennett, her heart was still racing.

Now, showered and fed so she wasn't hangry, she had time to look into Club TEN29. The name sounded familiar, and she'd originally assumed it was because of their concert with Tangled Royal, but something else was niggling at the back of her brain.

She plugged in the club's website and read through the information, impressed with everything she saw, from the classy look of the club to the detail and money put into the site itself. She moved on to the About page. There were three owners, Jason Dare, Tanner Grayson, and the man she'd met, Landon Bennett. Her stomach flipped at the thought of him.

She scanned the words, scrolling past the full-color pictures of each man, though she'd be lying if she said she didn't stop and stare at Landon, until she and came to a dedication at the end.

Club TEN29 is named in memory of Levi Bennett, who died in a tragic accident on October 29, 2009. And beneath that was the photograph of a guy who appeared almost identical to a younger Landon.

And suddenly she knew why Club TEN29 sounded familiar, and it had nothing to do with their hosting of Tangled Royal. Her pulse pounded hard and nausea threatened, but before she panicked completely, she Googled her brother's name—Victor Clark, Club TEN29, and bomb threat – and prayed she was wrong with the connection she'd made. Unfortunately, the articles came up, backing her hunch.

She picked up her cell and called Ellie, who lived in an apartment upstairs. "Come down," she said when her friend answered.

She knew Ellie would hear the urgency in her voice, and sure enough, Ellie was banging on her door soon after. "What's wrong?" she asked the second after Vivi let her inside.

Like Vivi, Ellie had showered and was now wearing a sundress but her hair was still damp.

"Remember on the way home from Owen's, I said the club name sounded familiar?" Vivi asked.

Ellie nodded. "Come sit. You look green. Why is the name familiar?"

Vivi swallowed back the bile that threatened and

followed her friend to her sofa. They sat down and Ellie waited for Vivi to talk.

"My brother, Victor, killed Landon's twin in a horrible hazing gone wrong back in college."

Ellie's eyes opened wide. "Your brother who got out and then was thrown back in prison for terrorizing some guys?"

Vivi nodded. "He went after Landon's partner, Tanner Grayson." Thanks to the articles she'd pulled up, Vivi was now too familiar with the details. "He vandalized their club. He tried to attack Tanner's girlfriend. He called in a bomb threat, which is a federal offense, by the way, and told the cops the bar was serving underage kids, causing a raid." She blinked back tears. "He killed Landon's twin." She repeated the worst of the crimes because that was the one that mattered the most.

She'd spent so much time trying to disassociate herself from her brother. When Victor had been arrested for hazing and manslaughter, Vivi, sadly, hadn't been shocked that her brother had been capable of hurting someone so badly. He'd been in and out of trouble for years, each time subjecting him to a beating from her father.

Unable to take it anymore, her mother divorced him during that horrific time, and the press had been so relentless, Vivi and her mother had legally changed their last names back to her mom's maiden name, Zane, and moved out of state. At that point she hadn't had a good relationship with her brother in years. He'd resented her so-called status with her father and treated her like shit anyway, so she hadn't contacted him in prison and vice versa.

When he'd been released, he'd claimed to want a relationship, and they'd met for lunch. The next day he called her because he'd been arrested again. Obviously he'd been setting her up to bail him out if he got caught. He'd rambled about being accused of phoning in a bomb threat to a club and assault, among other things.

She'd hung up on him, and though she'd heard information on the news, including the club's name, she hadn't followed the case. She'd wanted nothing to do with her sibling. But she didn't think Landon Bennett would care about her lack of a relationship with Vic. Because of her mere association, he and his partners would want nothing to do with her.

"Once Landon finds out I'm Vic's sister, I can kiss any chance at the residency goodbye. I can't take the job." Her stomach hurt at the loss of such huge potential but not as much as it twisted in pain for Landon, whose brother was dead.

Ellie pulled at a nonexistent thread on her dress. "Or … you don't ever have to tell him."

Whipping her head up, Vivi stared at her friend. "What? No. I'm not going to lie about something that huge. I couldn't live with myself."

"I didn't think you could," her friend said softly. "I just had to offer it as a solution because you know that's what Owen would tell you to do."

"Fuck Owen. He only cares about money. Not about what I want or about people's lives."

"Amen."

Vivi met Ellie's gaze. "Fucking Victor. He's a terror even when he isn't part of my life," she said, as she watched her dreams shatter before she'd ever grasped them in her hand.

"You know I support you, right? Whatever you decide, I'm in your corner."

Ellie squeezed her hand and Vivi smiled. "You're such a good friend. I can't believe we met at the gym only one year ago. I feel like I've known you forever."

Ellie gave her a smile. "Fate works in weird ways. I needed a job and you needed an assistant." Vivi had been working in a coffee shop during the day and singing when she could find work at night. She'd managed to pay Ellie very little to handle her website and help with social media, but she'd kept her job at a clothing store until Vivi started to get more steady singing work.

Eventually Owen had been in one of the venues

where she'd been singing, heard her, and offered to sign her on the spot. Even then, she'd said she'd think about it and sent his contract over to her mom.

"Do it," Ellie said, gesturing to Vivi's cell. "It's not going to get any easier.

With a sigh, Vivi picked up her phone, called Owen, and left a message, turning down the residency offer.

Then, knowing he'd call back screaming, she shut her phone off, pulled a pint of ice cream from the freezer, and shared the treat with her best friend.

LANDON AND JASON sat at the gym, where Tanner was fighting in the ring. Ever since Tanner had hooked up with Scarlett Davis, an assistant district attorney, and since Victor Clark had gone back to jail, Tanner's anger issues seemed well under control. Where he used to fight at the gym to channel his aggression, lately it seemed he took more enjoyment in the sport.

They still showed up to support Tanner, and in truth, old habits died hard. They wanted to be here if something triggered their friend's anger, although Landon didn't see that as an issue any longer. Which meant they could focus on something other than watching Tanner kick someone's ass in the ring.

"So how'd the visit with the viral girl go?" Jason

asked, one eye on Tanner.

Landon felt the beginnings of a stupid grin on his face, and clearly Jason caught it, too, because he burst out laughing.

"I knew it would happen sooner or later. Tanner did, too." Jason grinned.

"I don't know what the fuck you're talking about." Because hedging was better than admitting that Landon had taken one look at Vivienne ... he preferred Vivi because it suited her ... and he'd fallen ass over teakettle, as his grandmother used to say. He'd thought it was as stupid an expression as Jason falling for Faith in a few short days and Tanner for Scarlett just as quickly. Now he understood. He wanted to get to know this woman.

"But it went well. I know her agent is completely on board, and though she tried to play it cool, she's interested." In more than just the summer residency, he thought.

And that feeling was completely mutual.

He'd been sitting in that office listening to the asshole agent try and blow smoke up his ass about how much money his client was worth when she'd come rushing inside. Her hair was pulled up in a bun, that lush body encased in Spandex, and he'd had a good look at breasts made to fit in his hand and nipples that had puckered under his gaze.

His dick had hardened at the sight.

And then he'd had his first glimpse of her beautiful face, up close and personal. Gorgeous brown eyes the color of hot chocolate framed by porcelain skin, a sprinkling of freckles on the bridge of her nose, and dimples on either side of sexy lips made for kissing.

He'd been blindsided by not just her beauty but her strength of character. She'd stood up to her agent, letting him know the details of the contract were up to *her*. She didn't seem to go for the money grab the man clearly had on his mind. More than a point in her favor.

"And you're into her," Jason said. "Because I've been talking for the last few minutes and you haven't heard one word I've said. I brought her up and you got lost." He chuckled to himself.

Landon rolled his eyes but he couldn't deny his friend was right. His cell rang and he pulled it from his pocket, glancing at the screen. Vivi's agent. His pulse picked up speed as he envisioned having her within touching distance all summer long.

He hit the accept button. "Bennett."

"Mr. Bennett, it's Owen Rhimes. I'm afraid I have bad news for you. Vivienne asked me to turn down your offer."

"What? Why?" He had to admit he was floored. From the chemistry between them, which had been undeniable, to the generosity of the offer ... he hadn't expected her to reject him outright. Negotiate? Yeah, that he'd anticipated.

Jason glanced at him, brows furrowed.

Landon shook his head.

"I have to admit I'm taken off guard myself. She'd been clear about wanting to stay in town. I even had a list of wants for her. But she wouldn't let me negotiate. Just gave me a firm no." The man sounded frustrated, too.

"Thank you." Frowning, he disconnected the call.

"What's up?" Jason asked.

Landon shifted in the metal chair he'd been sitting on for too long. "She turned down the summer residency offer." Dammit.

"What are you going to do about it? We can meet up and brainstorm someone else," Jason said as Tanner stepped out of the ring along with his sparring partner, who stomped away, pissed he'd lost.

Landon clearly recalled the interested look in her eyes when she'd first seen him and the flicker of excitement at the mention of the summer residency. Oh, she'd tried to hide it and act professional, to not tip her hand so she'd have leverage to negotiate, because she'd acted like she could take it or leave it ... but he'd seen and sensed how badly she'd wanted the gig.

"No. Nobody else. She's our first choice, and I'm going to talk to her and see why she'd turn down such a lucrative contract."

A decent agent wouldn't share his client's address, but he had a feeling Owen Rhimes wasn't as decent of an agent as he claimed to be. Then again, Vivi was an unknown talent, so she'd probably taken what she could get.

He called Owen back. "I'd like to talk to your client. Any chance you can tell me where to find her?"

"Well ... it would really be unethical of me to share her personal information, Mr. Bennett."

He glanced at Jason, who was watching him, amusement in his gaze. Even Tanner had figured out what was going on if his smirk was anything to go by.

"Really? That's too bad, because I think I can convince her to take the deal, and I know that's what we both want."

He heard the pause at the other end of the line, and he didn't really believe the man was struggling with his conscience; rather Landon figured Owen was trying to make him believe it.

A few seconds later, Landon had Vivi's address in hand. He'd give her tonight to think about the what she'd given up ... and he'd be on her doorstep in the morning.

✧   ✧   ✧

WHEN THE KNOCK sounded on Vivi's door the next day, she wasn't surprised. She hadn't thought Owen was going to let this go with a voicemail message and a follow-up phone call. Even so, Vivi had made up her mind. After what her brother had done to Landon and his partners, it wasn't fair for her to take the job. She also had no intention of revealing who she was to them and subjecting herself to their disdain. She didn't know Landon, but she knew she'd fall apart if he turned his rightful hurt and anger on her.

Preparing herself to deal with Owen, she flung the door open and came face-to-face with Landon instead. "Oh."

Wearing a pair of jeans and a collared tee shirt, he looked sexy instead of uptight like Owen when he wore a similar outfit. The top two buttons were open, leaving his tanned chest and a sprinkling of dark hair visible for her to see, and she imagined her hand settled there, her fingers running over his skin.

She pulled her gaze upward and met his stare, glad she was dressed in jeans and a tee shirt of her own. Being fully clothed put her on more equal footing than her skimpy gym wear. And it covered her body's instant reaction to merely looking at him.

"Hi." He greeted her with a grin.

"Hi." She didn't ask how he'd found her. She knew Owen would cross any boundaries to get her to take this job.

"Can we talk?" he asked.

It would be rude if she said no without hearing him out, so she nodded. "Sure. Come on in." She led him into her small apartment, all too aware of the shabby furniture and chipped paint on the walls.

It wasn't going to make sense to him why she lived in such a run-down place and was turning down his offer. She gritted her teeth and hoped she could find a way out, short of explaining who she was.

"We can sit here." She led him to the sofa and they sat across from each other. She clasped her hands together, trying to hide her nerves. "So what can I do for you?"

His addictive grin did funny things to her insides, and she trembled beneath that seductive gaze.

"I'm not here to ask why you said no to my offer," he said, his words taking her by surprise. "But I am going tell you all the reasons you should say yes." He leaned back against the sofa and held her stare. "My partners and I have been through hell these last couple of months."

She stiffened in shock. Of all the things she'd expected, him confiding in her hadn't been on the agenda. "I'm sorry," she said, twisting her fingers

34

together.

"When we were younger, we went through an ... unimaginable experience and my twin died." He paused, glancing away, his eyes clouding over. "Actually he was killed."

Jesus. "Landon, I'm so sorry." Her throat swelled and the truth swirled around in her head, but she knew better than to admit it now.

He shot her an appreciative glance while running a hand through his hair, messing the long strands. "Then, a few months ago, the bastard who killed him got out of prison and came after us," he said, jaw tight. "I don't want to get into the specifics, but the point is the club took a hit. People stopped coming in. The Tangled Royal concert was a way to bring the customers back and to make them feel safe."

"I assume it worked?" she asked.

He nodded. "To a point. But summer is coming. People go away, leave for the Hamptons, the Jersey Shore. We want to keep our numbers up, and we believe you're the key to that."

She stared at her ugly flowered sofa. "I'm sure there are other artists who could step in and accomplish the same thing."

But despite her words, she had to admit he was persuasive. She wanted to help him, if for no other reason than to undo a small measure of the problems and pain her brother had caused, and she couldn't deny the money he offered would help her personally and the job itself would build her brand and get her name out to the public.

He leaned in closer, as if sensing he was getting to her. "Your numbers on YouTube prove how much people like you. Imagine building your presence on a stage in one of the biggest up-and-coming clubs in Manhattan?"

The idea was exciting and everything she wanted, but she felt guilty accepting knowing who she was. "I don't know."

He looked around her apartment, and she didn't have to follow his gaze to know what he saw. Peeling walls, stained carpet, scuffed floors.

"I assume you aren't making much now. Have you looked at the contract?" he asked in a nonjudgmental voice.

She shook her head. She hadn't wanted to be tempted by a lucrative amount of money.

He narrowed his gaze in confusion, as if he didn't understand her, but continued. "We're offering you an apartment above the club for the summer. The place is immaculate. A fully stocked fridge with anything you want inside it and weekly deliveries. We'll cover your incidentals in addition to pay per performance. And your manager mentioned you want to record your music. I'm willing to cover your studio fees for the duration of the residency. And I'm assuming you have debt? The salary will help alleviate that without you having to pay rent and utilities."

Oh, God. He was offering the world, at least the world she wanted. "Why me?" She blurted out the main question circling her mind. "I mean there are any number of artists in the city. Why are you offering all of this to me?"

He blew out a breath and she sensed his internal struggle, as if he had more to say than he wanted to admit. "I used to play. Piano, guitar, whatever."

She blinked in surprise.

"I know talent," he said with a shrug. "I can feel that you're meant for big things and I can help. It's a leg up. Promoters and better managers than Owen will stop by Club TEN29 over the course of the summer. Do you have any idea what this can do for your career? Not to mention how much you'll be helping us out?"

She hung her head and sighed. How did she take this job knowing what she did about their connection? Yet how did she turn it down?

When she hesitated again, he waited until she met his gaze. "Now I have to ask why. I saw the initial interest in your eyes. What changed your mind?"

She dug her nails into her skin. "I … I don't think

I deserve it."

He eased in closer until his legs touched hers. "Of course you deserve it. You just have to reach out and take the chance. Accept the opportunity. Help me and my partners," he said, his tone imploring her to say yes.

She blew out a long breath, doing her best to ignore the heat of his body so close to hers. He was distracting her with his masculine presence and scent, and his argument was compelling and alluring.

He added to her confusion by taking her hand in his bigger, warmer one. "My club needs you. My partners and I need you. And we're giving you back so much in return." He turned those gorgeous blue eyes on her. "Say yes, Vivi."

Her internal struggle wavered. Bottom line, she needed this job as much as he said they needed her, and she reasoned that it was only a temporary gig. A few months and she could pay off her bills, finance her career, and move on without them knowing the truth.

"Yes," she finally said, hoping if he ever found out who she really was, he'd understand why she'd withheld the information. With luck, the truth would never be brought to light.

✧   ✧   ✧

LANDON WIPED DOWN the bar, happy to be making himself useful in his own place of business. As usual, his thoughts strayed to Vivi. After she'd agreed to the summer residency, he'd immediately had the contract updated to include her studio fee and other things Owen had insisted upon that were minimal, at least as far as Landon was concerned.

Although he hadn't heard from her in the week since their meeting, he'd received the signed contract yesterday and had breathed a sigh of relief. He didn't know what it was about her that intrigued him so much, but he'd wanted her locked into their club for the summer.

Tied to him.

Now that he knew he'd be seeing her often, he could definitely make his play. She interested him in a way no woman ever had, and he knew better than to ignore such a strong attraction when he'd never thought fate would give him the same happiness his friends had found.

Since losing his twin, it was as if a part of him was missing, and he understood he'd never replace or fill that hole in both his heart and his soul. But he wouldn't mind discovering some form of that happiness in his personal life.

They had three weeks before the summer, which didn't give her much time to pull an act together for her performance. If it hadn't been for Vic taking up the bulk of his time and concentration, he would have put this into motion sooner ... but then maybe he wouldn't have seen the video of Vivi. Everything worked out for the best or so he believed.

He tossed the damp rag into a bin behind the bar, wondering when Vivi would come by and check out her new digs.

"Uncle Landon!" His ten-year-old nephew ran around the bar and barreled into Landon, wrapping his scrawny arms around his waist.

"Hey, buddy!" he said to LJ, named after Landon's twin, Levi.

Amber Davis, the woman he assumed would have been his sister-in-law had Levi lived and the mother of his nephew, leaned against the bar and grinned. "Surprise!"

"Amber, what brings you to the city?" he asked.

A sheepish expression etched her features. "As you know, LJ and I are staying with your parents in Connecticut until we can move into our new house, and since he's going to be traveling with them while I get settled, I thought I'd familiarize him with Manhattan."

He shook his head. "Worried mom, hmm? He's going to be fine with my folks. I promise. And you will get a head start on your new life."

He and his partners, Amber's good friends and

LJ's pseudo uncles, had finally convinced Amber to let them buy her a house near Landon's parents, in Connecticut. She planned to go back to school to get her degree in education, having dropped out ten years ago during her freshman year after finding out she was pregnant. After Levi had died.

She grinned. "Thanks to you and the guys."

She glanced at her son. "So this is Uncle Landon's club. You won't be here when it's busy at night, but I'm sure you'll spend some time here with Uncle Jason and Uncle Tanner, too."

His eyes lit up at the mention of his uncles. "Are they here?" he asked.

Landon nodded. "Up in the office. Why don't you take the elevator." He gestured to the elevator across the way that opened directly into the offices upstairs. "Hit two and it goes right to the floor."

"Cool! Then can we go to that place you promised, Mom? With frozen hot chocolate?"

She nodded. "Serendipity. Sure, honey." He and Amber watched him run to the elevator and hit the button. As soon as he was in the enclosed space and the door shut, they faced each other.

"You're worried about him missing you this summer?" Landon assumed that was what was on Amber's mind.

She sighed. "I'm more worried about me missing

him. I thought if I got a sense for where he'd be, I'd feel better." She gestured to a low table and chairs, and he followed her over, pulling out her seat.

After she settled, he lowered himself into his chair. "Look, for a long time, it's just been you and LJ, and your parents in Florida. It's going to take time to adjust to a life where he travels to visit relatives." He reached out and placed his hand over hers. "It's going to be great. I can't wait to drive up and play ball with him this summer. And maybe we can convince you to have a barbeque for all of us." He winked at her. "Relax, okay?"

She blew out a shaky breath. "I agree or I wouldn't have left the Sunshine State and come here to start over. I want him to be closer to Levi's family. To you."

He grinned. He appreciated his friendly relationship with Amber. Despite the fact that he looked exactly like his twin, there had never been any sexual vibes between them, and for that he was grateful. She was family, pure and simple.

"How about joining us for some frozen hot chocolate?" she asked.

"I could be persuaded." He didn't have a sweet tooth but knew it would mean a lot to her, plus he'd be able to spend more time with LJ.

"Great!" She rose and pulled him up and into a hug. "I don't know what I would have done without the three of you all these years. And your parents." His mom and dad had accepted Amber and LJ from the moment she told them she was pregnant with Levi's baby.

"We're always here for you," he said, about to let her go.

"Umm, excuse me. I came by to check out the club. I called earlier and Jason Dare told me to come over," a familiar female voice said.

Vivi.

He jerked out of the embrace, turning to see the woman he couldn't get out of his head watching him with a curious expression on her pretty face.

He'd been waiting for her to show up and make arrangements to move in, and now she was here. He took in her outfit, a flirty spring dress with a pair of chunky-heeled mini boots, his gaze taking in her long legs and the flowered dress that hugged her curves.

He couldn't stop the slow grin of appreciation at the sight of her. But he did not want her to get the wrong idea about his relationship with Amber.

Chapter Three

WHEN VIVI WALKED into Club TEN29, the last thing she expected to see was Landon wrapped in another woman's embrace.

Were they together? She wondered but reminded herself it didn't matter. Given her family tree, she wouldn't get involved with him, not knowing Vic was her brother. But they'd each given off some strong sexual tension, and she'd be shocked if Landon had a girlfriend. It would state something negative about his character that would be disappointing.

"Vivi," he said in a gruff, pleased voice.

"Hi." She pulled her handbag closer around her. "I can come back if it's a bad time."

"Not at all. Come on in." He stepped away from the woman in question and toward Vivi, gesturing for her to come closer. "Vivi, I'd like you to meet Amber Davis. Amber, this is Vivi Zane. She's going to be our star singing act this summer."

"Nice to meet you," Amber said, a smile on her pretty face. "I'm going to have to find a way to come see you sing! Assuming I can find a babysitter."

Babysitter? Was Landon a father? Vivi's stomach twisted with an emotion she didn't want to name.

"You will," he assured her. "You'll meet people and it'll all fall into place."

Totally lost, Vivi just stood there, listening.

"Well, I'm going to go upstairs and talk to the guys. I'll come back when LJ is ready to go to Serendipity?" Amber cocked her head to the side, her blonde hair falling over her shoulder, and Landon nodded.

Obviously they had plans. Vivi did her best to shake off the jealousy she was feeling. Jealousy she had no right or reason to experience. She barely knew Landon and he was off-limits anyway.

"Bye, Vivi. Nice to meet you," Amber said as she strode off.

"Bye."

Once they were alone, Landon met Vivi's gaze, giving her one of his megawatt smiles that made her stomach flutter with too much awareness. "Jason didn't mention you were coming by."

"Is it a problem?" she asked.

"No, of course not. I'm glad to see you."

He sounded sincere, yet she felt as though she was getting mixed messages. The attraction between them was definitely still there, but it wasn't appropriate if he

46

was in a relationship with the other woman.

"I'm sorry if I was interrupting a private moment."

He waved a hand, dismissing her words. "Amber is … the closest thing to a sister-in-law I'll ever have. She's my nephew's mom."

Vivi blinked. "You have another brother?" He'd already told her about losing his twin.

"No, no other brother." He shoved his hands into the front pockets of his pants. "Amber was Levi's college girlfriend. She got pregnant before he died and found out about the baby after he was gone."

"Oh my God." Vivi placed a hand on her churning stomach. Her brother had killed a man and left a child without a father. Could this situation get any worse?

"Are you okay? You're pale." Obviously concerned, Landon put a hand on her shoulder.

"I–" She didn't know what she was except sick at heart.

"Come sit." He slid his hand farther around her.

Dizzy, she let him lead her to a chair and lowered herself into it. Knowing she had to pull herself together, she drew deep, slow breaths.

"Can I get you a glass of water?" He knelt down in front of her, concern on his handsome face.

She shook her head. "I'm sorry. I didn't eat this morning and it just hit me," she lied.

God, the damage her brother had caused Landon

and his family ... she could never make up for it. Saying yes to this opportunity was a mistake. It didn't matter that the money would help her personally, she'd done it mostly because he'd talked her into it, saying she'd be helping them. "Landon–"

"Vivi–"

She managed a laugh, which alleviated the awful feeling in her stomach. "You first."

His warm, seductive blue eyes held on to hers, drawing her in. "I want to show you around," he said, changing the subject. "Let you see where you'll be working, and then I can take you upstairs, where there's a refrigerator and food. You can grab something to eat, check out the offices and then the apartment that'll be yours."

She blew out a breath. "About that–"

"You have no idea how excited my partners are that you said yes," he said before she could continue. "We're already planning a huge advertising campaign around you, we've hired a PR firm, and since we have three weeks for you to get ready, we're giving you access during the day for rehearsals."

They'd already heavily invested in her summer residency, she thought, her heart thudding hard. These men and their business were counting on her, leaving her unable to bail on them because of her personal guilt. All she could do was perform her heart out and hope they never found out who she really was.

"Here I am rambling about my excitement. So what did you want to tell me?" he asked.

She shook her head. "Nothing. It wasn't important. I'm feeling better, so how about that grand tour?"

He winked and wrapped his big, warm hand around hers and pulled her to her feet. "Come on. The bar is obvious but come check out the stage." They walked toward the large area. "There's an expansive dance floor and a stage that will hold you and your band. And the baby grand is yours to use."

She glanced at him curiously. "Do you use it?" She walked over and ran her fingers over the keyboard. "I mean, you mentioned that you used to play." She glanced at his hands and long fingers made for playing and other seductive pleasures.

He immediately curled them into fists at his sides, dispelling that erotic notion. "I don't play anymore. Haven't in years. Let's go to the apartment," he said roughly.

Taking that as forbidden territory, which she respected given how many secrets she had of her own, she nodded. "I'd love to see."

He placed his hand on the small of her back and led her to the elevator Amber had taken earlier. Even through the fabric of her dress, his palm felt like a brand against her skin.

They stepped out into a small hallway, and he pulled a set of keys from his pocket, opened the door, and let them inside.

She took in the gorgeous chrome, black, and white décor and her eyes opened wide. There was a wall unit with a built-in bar, comfortable-looking leather sofas, and reclining chairs across from a large-screen television hanging on the wall. The walls were painted a soft white without a chip or crack to be seen.

The kitchen wasn't large but she didn't need it to be. There was adequate counter space with a gorgeous granite top in a mixed swirl of white and black, and a microwave for easy prep, which was all she did, considering until now she hadn't had the money for gourmet meals. Pasta, soup and sandwich, and finished. But the granite gleamed as did the shiny silver hardware on the white cabinets.

A place like this was heaven to a girl like her. "Oh my God, this is beautiful." Knowing she was gawking, she turned to face him. "You're sure you don't need this for someone else?" She couldn't believe they were offering her such a luxurious place to stay as part of her contract. Sure, she'd heard of such a thing, but she'd never expected it for herself.

He rolled his broad shoulders. "We don't need it. We all took turns staying here when we had late nights back when the guys were single. Jason is married and would much rather go home to his wife, and Tanner is engaged. End result is the same."

"And you?" She eyed him curiously. "You don't want an easy place to crash?" *Or a place to bring women?* she wondered. It would be very convenient for single men to have an apartment upstairs.

He leaned against the bar, looking at ease and sexy. She loved his casual look, a pair of dark jeans and a light blue faded tee shirt, accentuating those blue eyes.

"I have a three-bedroom nearby. It's a renovated warehouse that's now an oversized apartment. I can be home in five minutes, no problem."

"Okay then."

"We moved our things out and had the place professionally cleaned. It's all yours," he assured her. "Want to check out the *bedroom*?"

The word dropped between them like a bomb ready to go off, because despite her having drawn an invisible line she knew better than to cross, she wanted to get to know him better. To let her sexual attraction for him show. Unfortunately, she couldn't do it.

He, however, had other ideas, because he extended his hand, and unable to resist despite the lectures she'd given herself thus far, she placed her palm inside his, and he led her to the bedroom in the far corner of the apartment.

✧   ✧   ✧

THE MINUTE LANDON led Vivi into the small room, which was taken up mostly by the bed, he knew he was in trouble. Dirty thoughts immediately filled his mind of himself and Vivi tangled together on the mattress. His hands wrapped in her long hair, his cock deep inside her body. At the thought, the anatomy in question threatened to make itself known. He cleared his throat and turned away until he had himself under control. Then he spun back around.

"So this is the bedroom," she said, looking around the immaculate space.

"Yes, it is. Feel free to put your own touches on it for as long as you're here." The decorator had pulled together an apartment for three single men.

She treated him to a generous smile. "Thank you."

Knowing he'd be tempting himself and not caring, he stepped closer until her feminine fragrance filled his nostrils. They stared at each other for a long, charged moment, desire he couldn't escape building inside him.

She met his gaze and her lips parted. It wasn't an invitation, but her eyes still held his, and she wasn't backing away either.

He slid his hand behind her neck, cupping her soft skin. "I know I'm your boss, so no pressure," he said as he applied a bit to her skin. "But I want to kiss you."

She paused. Looked up at him. Then rose onto her toes. His mouth met hers. Warm and willing, her soft lips glided against his and his entire body came alive. He tightened his grip on her neck as he slid his tongue into her waiting mouth. She tasted sweet and he deepened the kiss, wanting more of her. With a moan, her body leaned against his, her breasts pressing against his chest.

Their tongues meshed and mingled. Their harsh breathing filled the room. The kiss went on and he was in no rush to end the moment. But suddenly she gasped and pulled away.

"We shouldn't," she said, brushing her damp lips with her hand.

"Because…?"

She swallowed hard. "I just … I need to focus on my work," she said, turning away so he couldn't see her face.

He narrowed his gaze, wondering if something more was at play. A woman didn't kiss him like she did, then back off that easily. But he also wasn't going to push her. He'd see how things between them played out during her time here and take his cues from her. Which didn't mean he wouldn't play up the charm and test her resolve.

"I think the apartment will work out well." She

headed for the door.

"Do you need help moving in?"

"I've got it but thank you," she said in a strained voice.

"Who's helping?" he persisted.

"Well, Ellie. Owen wouldn't get his hands dirty moving my clothing over. It's fine. We've got it. She's borrowing her parents' car."

He rolled his eyes. "I'll be over at eight a.m. tomorrow and we'll get you moved in."

He wasn't going to leave the two women to drag all her things alone back and forth up to the apartment.

"*We'll* get me moved in?"

He grinned. "I've got partners, don't I? All you need to worry about is packing your things up. We'll handle the rest."

"But—"

He placed a finger to her lips, and damned if her eyes didn't darken with desire. She might be focused on her career, but she was interested in him as well.

"No buts," he told her. "You're ours to take care of now."

THAT KISS BLEW Vivi's mind and stayed there while she wrapped plastic garbage bags over the clothes in

54

her closet so she could just rehang them in her new one. She boxed up everything else. There wasn't all that much. She'd be buying stage clothes for this residency with her advance paycheck. And memories of Landon's sexy mouth on hers kept her up all night and well into the morning.

It wasn't just the talent of those lips and that tongue; no, it was the explosive chemistry she'd never shared with anyone before. Vivi had had relationships in her past, and they'd always ended on an easy note, including the last one with the drummer in her band. The attraction, what little there usually was with past men, tended to fade away along with the desire for her to remain attached. But she'd never experienced a kiss that had exploded throughout her entire being and taken her out of her own mind.

She'd come close to crawling up Landon's hard body, tackling him, and ending up on the bed that'd been close by. But her ever-present guilty conscience had chosen that moment to rear its head. He deserved a woman who could come to him free of ugly entanglements in their past. And that wasn't her.

So she'd broken the kiss and tried to leave, but he'd been insistent on helping her, and now he was coming over early this morning for her move into the club apartment. Where she'd see him every day and her body would react to him every waking minute.

She rose early and headed downstairs, buying a Dunkin' Box O' Joe that included ten cups of coffee, along with a dozen donuts for her, Ellie, Landon, and his partners.

At eight on the dot, the men showed up, to Vivi's surprise, with their women, too.

"We're here to help," a curvy blonde with a sweet smile said. "I'm Faith Dare. And you must be Vivi." She extended her hand and Vivi shook it. "This is my husband, Jason." She gestured to a handsome man with brown hair and a scruff of beard. "Tanner Grayson and his fiancee, Scarlett," Faith said, continuing with the introductions to all good-looking people, as Vivi took each person's hand in turn.

"Where's Landon?" she asked, glancing over their shoulders.

"He stopped at Dunkin'. He thinks he had to bribe us all to help but we wanted to come," Scarlett said.

Vivi laughed. "I already did the same thing. There's a box in the kitchen and a dozen donuts. But since I only planned on the guys, his coffee run will help. Especially if you're all big caffeine drinkers."

"Oh, trust me, we are," Tanner said.

"Then let's go to the kitchen." She gestured a step or two away in her little apartment, and they all congregated around the counter. "I picked up cups from the store. Make yourselves at home." Vivi moved

56

aside so everyone could pour their coffee.

"Door's open. I'm coming in!" Ellie stepped inside and Vivi met her at the apartment entrance. "What is going on?" her friend asked, looking at the crowd of people in Vivi's small apartment.

"Apparently Landon decided I needed help moving, and he brought his partners. And they brought their women." Vivi tipped her head toward the couples.

"A real family affair," Ellie said with a snicker. "So, care to introduce me?"

Before Vivi could do just that, Landon arrived with the same box of coffee and donuts Vivi had bought. She took one look at him in his jeans and tee shirt, biceps visible, his hair still slightly damp, a grin on his handsome face, and the lady parts he'd woken up yesterday came back to life. She didn't glance down at her tee shirt, not wanting to draw attention to her now perky nipples.

"Come in," she said with a sweep of her hand. "Just put the coffee and donuts on the counter next to mine."

He grinned at her statement. "I guess great minds think alike. But I'm sure we'll drink and eat it all while we're loading up cars."

Since the apartment above the club was furnished, she didn't have to worry about moving heavy pieces, and besides, the crap items she owned weren't worth keeping. She'd already made a deal with her landlord. He'd keep the furnishings and she'd forgo her security deposit.

Landon headed to the kitchen area and her gaze fell to his backside. His jeans molded to his firm ass, and she wondered what it would be like to cup her hands around him and–

"Oh my God, you want to fuck him!" Ellie said. At least she'd kept her voice to a whisper, but it still sounded too loud for Vivi's taste.

"Shhh!" She glared at her friend. "What's wrong with you? All his family and friends are right there." She tipped her head.

"Are you going to act on that attraction?" Ellie asked, eyes wide and curious.

Vivi shook her head. "No." Not again, she thought. That first time had been a slipup. One she couldn't make again, and she hadn't told her friend about the kiss, either. "Now hush. He's coming back."

Landon returned, coffee cup in hand. "Are you ready to load up?"

She nodded. "The clothes are still on hangers, covered with garbage bags for protection. Everything else is boxed up. Honestly, there isn't that much. We didn't need all these people."

He chuckled. "Want to know a secret?" He leaned

in close, the scent of his aftershave overwhelming her in the best possible way. "The women are nosey. They wanted to meet you and they didn't want to wait for you to get settled at the club."

She was kind of flattered. "That's sweet and we've already been introduced. But I don't think we need them to help me move."

Landon leaned a hip against the radiator by the wall. "Tell you what. Point me to the boxes and clothes, I'll grab the guys, and you can indulge their curiosity and talk with them for a while." His glance included Ellie but lingered on Vivi.

"Listen to him!" Faith, who Vivi hadn't realized had joined them, said.

The bubbly blonde struck Vivi as the more outgoing one of the two. Scarlett seemed the more watch-and-assess-before-acting type.

Realizing she was outvoted as far as her helping, Vivi directed the men to the bedroom for the clothing and pointed out the boxes at the other end of her living room.

"So, you are going to love living above the club," Faith told her.

"Agreed." Scarlett came up beside Ellie, who watched with amusement.

"Rumor has it Tanner and Scarlett's first get-together was in that apartment," Faith said, then took a sip of her coffee.

"Faith!" Scarlett blushed a bright red.

"Don't worry. We bought all new bedding and sheets for you." Faith grinned and Scarlett rolled her eyes, obviously used to her uninhibited personality.

"Umm, I'm not sure what to say to that." Vivi didn't want to imagine the other couple in her soon-to-be bed. "But I am really excited to start this new phase of my life."

"We saw your video. You're amazing," Scarlett said, then took a huge bite of a chocolate-frosted donut.

"See? I told you." Ellie grinned. "She's going to be huge one day."

Faith nodded. "I don't doubt it. Jason said Landon couldn't take his eyes off you in that video the first time he saw it."

Vivi blushed at the thought. Clearly the women were trying to ... matchmake maybe. But they didn't know what she did about her and Landon's connection.

"I just think Landon and I have music in common. He told me he recognizes talent and that's why he wanted me for the club."

Faith narrowed her gaze. "Umm, if there's one thing the guys have in common, it's a love-at-first-sight kind of thing. And from what we heard, he's hooked on you."

Vivi glanced from Faith to Scarlett, who was nodding in agreement, sipping her coffee at the same time.

"Well, Landon and I barely know each other." Except for that amazing kiss.

"You will. You have all summer," Faith said with certainty.

"But don't let it freak you out. He's a great guy," Scarlett added. "Just give him a chance."

Ignoring them, Vivi continued with her points against any kind of personal relationship with Landon. "I'm working for all three partners, so mixing business and pleasure isn't smart," she told them.

"Well, not with Tanner and Jason, obviously they're taken, but Landon's fair game," Scarlett said. "There's nothing in your contract against … what? Fraternizing? Personal relationships?"

"Well no but–" Vivi looked to Ellie for help, but her friend merely raised her shoulders as if to say she didn't know how to help her out of the other women's pushy matchmaking.

"I think that's it," Landon said, walking into the apartment in the nick of time. "With three of us, it took no time to get Tanner's SUV loaded."

Vivi had told Ellie not to borrow her parents' SUV after Landon insisted on helping. "Is there room for us or should we get an Uber?"

"There's room, ladies. We also have Jason's car." Landon's gaze fell to Vivi. "You and Ellie can come with me in the SUV."

Faith and Scarlett looked at one another, then to Vivi, and Faith mouthed, "See?"

Vivi shook her head at the other women's certainty Landon had an agenda where she was concerned. There was no doubt in her mind Landon was just trying to make her feel comfortable.

Everyone filed out of her apartment, and Landon waited until just she and Ellie were left. "Would you like a few minutes alone before we leave?" he asked.

She glanced around her small, old apartment and shook her head. She had no sentimental attachment. It'd been a place to sleep. A pit stop on what she hoped was the road to something better.

"I'm good," she said, reaching for her purse and pulling out her keys. "Onward and upward."

"I'm all for that," Landon said.

"Me, too," Ellie said. With her new salary that kicked in when Vivi got her first paycheck, Ellie was also in the midst of looking for an apartment in a better neighborhood.

She marched out the door. Landon followed, and Vivi locked the door on her former rental, hoping that whatever lay ahead was better than what she was leaving behind.

✧ ✧ ✧

VIVI WAS DRESSED and ready for the day, and she planned to spend it downstairs familiarizing herself with the stage, the piano, and the acoustics. Excitement buzzed in her veins as Ellie joined her in the kitchen of her new apartment.

"I'll just grab coffee at a Starbucks on the way home. Last night was fun. Thanks for having me," she said.

Vivi nodded. "Any time." And she meant it. She loved hanging with her best friend, ordering in Chinese food, and binge-watching movies until they passed out.

They'd also shared a small bottle of Prosecco to celebrate all the new things that were happening for both of them. Because when good happened to Vivi, Ellie benefitted.

A knock sounded.

"I'll get it," Ellie said. "I'm on my way out anyway." She strode over and opened the door to find Landon standing in the doorway.

Though Vivi was surprised to see him, she couldn't deny the thrill that rushed through her at his arrival.

"Hi," Ellie said to him. "Oooh, flowers. Very nice."

Vivi stepped to the side so she could see around

Ellie to where Landon held a vase filled with beautiful wild blooms.

"They're for Vivi," he said with a grin, his gaze going beyond Ellie to where Vivi stood.

"Well, I didn't think they were for me," she said with a laugh. "I was just leaving." Ellie gestured to the big satchel hooked over her arm. "I slept over. Girlfriend pajama party, you know?"

He blinked, his expression blank. "No, I don't know. I don't have sisters."

"Well, it means we were celebrating Vivi's new gig and life." She turned back and said to Vivi, "I'll see you tomorrow morning at ten for clothes shopping, and the band will be here at two for a strategy meeting." She spun toward the door. "See you soon," she said to Landon, brushing past him as she walked out.

"Can I come in?" he asked.

"Of course." Vivi smiled and waved him inside.

He shut the door and walked over, handing her the flowers. "I thought this place could use some brightening up. It's pretty much been a bachelor pad, as I mentioned."

"Thank you!" She set them down on a coffee table in front of the sofa, where they could be seen by anyone who walked into the apartment. "I appreciate it."

She met his gaze, his blue eyes taking her in. She

64

could drown in those depths … if she let herself.

Instead she cleared her throat. "So I was wondering if it would be okay if I spent the afternoon downstairs. I want to get familiar with the piano and the venue."

"No need to ask. Make yourself at home. The club opens for business at six p.m. and closes at four a.m. Earlier hours are yours."

She nodded. "Works for me."

"I just wanted to let you know there's no need to be uncomfortable around me. You said you don't want to get involved and I respect that."

"I … well, thank you." She wasn't sure what else to say. He'd given her the easy out she'd hoped for. The one she'd needed, and yet her stomach twisted in disappointment. For as much as them keeping their distance was necessary, she wished she didn't have to let him go.

Chapter Four

LANDON DROVE HOME from dinner at his parents' house. Carrie and Samuel lived in the same home in Linton, Connecticut, where Landon and Levi had grown up, making Landon's trips there difficult each and every time. It wasn't just that his parents had kept most of Levi's things in his bedroom, but the entire house reminded Landon of all he'd lost. But Samuel and Carrie hadn't meant it as a shrine.

They had somehow managed to both keep living and to stay together despite their pain and grief, and to find enjoyment where they could. With their grandson moving nearby this summer, they were excited. It was all they'd talked about during dinner, and Landon had to admit that he was looking forward to being around while his nephew grew up. LJ was as close to Levi as Landon could get, and he wanted to be there for his twin's son.

He arrived back at the club, knowing he was in for some self-torture. He'd spent the two and a half weeks since moving Vivi into the apartment in a state of pure sexual frustration.

While she rehearsed on stage with her band, both in and out of costume, he'd been completely unprepared for the impact she had on him physically and emotionally. He spent his days sitting by the bar or up in his office with windows overlooking the stage, watching her sensual moves and listening to her sultry voice. She strutted around the platform like she was born to own the spotlight, and he had no doubt she was headed for stardom. He only hoped he survived the two months she spent here if he was forced to look and not touch.

Now he stood behind the bar drinking from a bottle of water. Tanner and Jason had spent the day with their women, though one or both of them might stop by later. And Landon knew he should head out since it was an off night for him. He had his big, empty, three-bedroom renovated warehouse turned into an apartment, waiting for him.

But Vivi sat at the piano, her fingers flying over the keys, a soft song on her lips. Lips he was dying to kiss. He could still taste her sweet flavor as it had exploded on his tongue, and he groaned. Shifting in his seat, he adjusted his rigid cock. He couldn't let this go on. He needed to push things a little and see if she was as into him as he was into her.

He strode through the empty club and made his

way down to the stage area and the piano on the side. Vivi caught sight of him and smiled, slowing her touch on the keys until she came to a stop completely.

"Mind if I join you?" he asked.

She slid over on the stool, making room. He sat down beside her. She wore a pair of skinny jeans and a cut-off shirt that exposed her belly and hung low on her shoulder. The one closest to him. The desire to kiss her bare skin, to glide his tongue along her delectable flesh was strong.

"How are things going?" he asked instead.

"Great! I love it here. The band sounds amazing, we've worked up a fabulous routine, and everything is wonderful. No complaints." Her wide grin lit up the darkened room.

"I'm glad. That song you were playing… It's beautiful. Did you write it?"

She nodded and glanced down to where his fingers lingered on the keys. Huh. He hadn't even realized he'd put them there. Something about her music pulled him in and took him to emotional places he hadn't felt in ages. Desires he hadn't let himself experience since his brother had died.

Her gaze slid to his. "You said you used to play piano."

He debated how much to reveal, then found himself talking. "I can hear music and repeat it from memory. Levi had the same ability. After he passed away, it felt wrong to perform." But Landon's fingers were still touching the keys.

An understanding expression on her pretty face, a compassionate look in her eyes, she began to play the same tune she'd been singing earlier, then stopped and waited.

Drawing a deep breath, his hands hovered on the ivories, his insides trembling. Then, in a different octave, he repeated her tune. Suddenly they were playing together, leaving him stunned. His fingers felt odd, rusty from disuse but at the same time, a peace flowed over him along with the sense that his brother was with him. Approving.

He stopped and met her gaze. "That was…"

"Incredible," she said, her eyes wide. "Your ability to play by ear is astounding."

He shrugged. "I didn't realize how much I missed it. Thank you." Reaching out, he tucked a strand of hair behind her ear and leaned toward her.

He paused, giving her an out if she wanted one, and when she didn't pull back, he leaned in and sealed his lips over hers. This time wasn't as slow and sensual. His body came alive just as his soul had moments before. Thanks to Vivi.

He kissed her hard and she responded, quickly scooting across the bench to get closer to him. Her fingers threaded through his hair and he reciprocated, tangling his fingers in her long strands. Tipping his head, he slid his tongue into her mouth, teeth clashing, desire exploding between them.

He pulled her over him so she straddled his waist, and he dropped a hand to her hips, holding on to her, their mouths never breaking contact. She rocked her sweet pussy into his dick, and it was all he could do to keep the bench upright as she writhed against him.

Suddenly a glass crashed behind them, the sound startling them both.

"Sorry, boss!" Paul, his main bartender, called from by the bar. "Just came in to do some inventory."

Vivi jumped, the noise ruining the moment and, if her stricken expression was any indication, any chance he had of getting her into bed in the near future.

"Oh my God. I… This … this never should have happened." She stared at him, lips damp, cheeks flushed and her hair definitely messed from his fingers.

"I can't say I regret it," he told her.

She swiped the back of her hand over her mouth. "But I do. We shouldn't do this. We *can't* do this."

She scrambled back, looking panicked, and he narrowed his gaze.

"Why not? We're two consenting adults. I don't understand the issue."

Laughter sounded from behind them, and he heard

Jason's and Tanner's voices, joining the bartender. Son of a bitch. The last thing Landon needed was another interruption.

"I'm going to go upstairs," Vivi said. "I'm sorry, Landon, but this can't happen again." She started to walk away but he wasn't ready for her to go.

"Wait," he called out.

She turned, her expression sad. "Yes?"

"I'm going to find out why you're running from me."

She shook her head, spun, and headed for the elevator, leaving him frustrated and confused.

He glanced at his partners and Paul, talking and laughing at the bar, and cursed them for interrupting and causing Vivi to overthink. Because when she got out of her own head, things between them were combustible, and he couldn't imagine why that alone would frighten her.

He curled his fingers into frustrated fists, his cock hard and annoyed with him. He needed to find out what was behind her reticence to get involved, because it was clear that something had her spooked. And that whatever was bothering her was clearly a hell of a lot more than her just being too busy with her career. And Landon liked her too much to pretend the chemistry and emotions that flowed between them didn't matter.

✧   ✧   ✧

VIVI RUSHED TO the elevator and up to her apartment, her breathing coming in harsh, shallow gasps and not because the kiss had knocked her on her ass. If they hadn't been interrupted, who knew how far she'd have gone with him in the middle of the club. She could really have ended up naked on the piano or on the floor. She'd been that lost in Landon.

What had she been thinking?

Clearly she hadn't been.

She clicked the lock on the door and slid to the floor, her thoughts in turmoil. In playing the piano tonight, Landon had bared his soul to her. He'd shared a part of himself that he'd closed off after his twin died ... at her brother's hands. She knew for sure that the hazing had been deliberate even if Levi's death hadn't been.

But Vic had never taken ownership or responsibility during the investigation or after his arrest, insisting the death had been an accident. But there was nothing accidental about putting rocks in a drunk man's backpack and forcing him to run the stairs. Or slapping him when he fell and hit his head.

There was no excusing anything her brother had done that night, and she'd never tried to pretend otherwise. Vic might be her sibling, but that was a blood tie she didn't want to acknowledge. And one she wished wouldn't matter to Landon and his partners.

But it would.

God, she shouldn't have let him talk her into saying yes to the summer residency. She'd been an idiot to agree. Every time they were together, they bonded in small but extremely meaningful ways, and he wouldn't have opened up to her if he knew the truth.

She had to tell him and, regardless of her contract, be willing to walk away if he and the other men wanted her gone. But she didn't have the guts to tell all three men together.

Tomorrow she'd text Landon and tell him they needed to talk. Meanwhile she planned to crawl into bed, pull the covers over her head, and pretend her life wasn't a mess and she wasn't about to lose things that mattered to her. A chance with Landon included.

"HEY, ASSHOLES. WHAT are you doing here tonight? Don't you have women to be with?" Landon strode over to the bar and glared at his friends.

Paul grimaced. "Sorry, boss. I dropped a glass."

"Yeah. It's fine." Landon met Jason's gaze first. "Faith kick you out?"

"Hey, just because Vivi ran out on you doesn't mean you should be a jackass to me."

His friend's grin merely served to piss him off even more. "Fuck off, man."

Tanner narrowed his gaze. "Okay, this is a lot more than a make-out session gone wrong. What gives?"

Landon slammed his hand on the counter. "Something's freaking her out and I haven't a fucking clue what it is."

"Have you tried … oh, I don't know, talking to her?" This from Jason.

Landon scowled at him. "Did you see her run out? I'm not going to go banging on her door when she's upset. Not without a plan," he muttered.

Tanner settled his ass on a barstool, leaning one elbow on the counter. "Let her settle down tonight, and tomorrow morning show up with food and the intent to talk." He shrugged. "Not sure why I need to do all the thinking around here," he said with a grin.

"Man's got a good idea. Much as I hate to admit it." Jason laughed. "A few months with a good woman and he's smart around the opposite sex." He walked over to Landon and placed a hand on his shoulder. "Go home, get some sleep, and deal with Vivi in the morning."

Landon nodded. He could use the opportunity to process the time he'd spent with Vivi. Playing the piano? That had been akin to revealing his innermost pain. His friends obviously hadn't heard the music or they'd have been a lot more curious about what had caused him to play and been way more somber than they'd been.

"I'm out of here," Landon said.

"Hang in there," Jason called out.

Without answering, Landon turned and walked out.

With a knot in her stomach, Vivi performed her morning routine, showering, washing her hair, and putting on makeup, well aware of what she had to do today. Tell Landon who she was related to. Blow up her world. And his.

She picked up her coffee cup at the same time her phone rang. Noticing her mother's number, she answered immediately. "Hi, Mom."

"Baby, put on the television," her mother said in a panicked voice. "Your brother's being interviewed on the Channel Seven morning show."

"What? Why?" Vivi immediately rushed to find the remote and turn on the TV.

"The previews said they were doing a piece on the rise of deadly college hazing incidents and they were going to talk to someone who had firsthand experience. A unique perspective from the perpetrator, even if the incident was over a decade ago."

Bile threatened to come up her throat. "Okay, I've got it on. Stay on with me." She gripped the phone and lowered herself onto the sofa in front of the big-screen television.

Her mother's worried breathing sounded on the other end of the phone. Finally the commercial ended and the interviewer came back on screen. Connie Lazarus, a familiar morning show staple, began to speak, and the screen flashed to the interview.

Vic sat in a prison uniform across from Connie, looking older than the last time she'd seen him, his frame big and bulky, his expression lacking any remorse. If anything, an amused smile lifted his lips, causing Vivi to shiver. She'd seen that look on his face before, and it had never boded well for anyone on the other end.

Connie crossed her legs and leaned in. "So, Mr. Clark, you're in prison for numerous crimes, but we're here to talk about hazing in particular."

She went on to mention various schools conducting investigations now, fraternities being suspended, and students who had passed away. "I'd like to discuss your perspective. What was going through your mind at the time you were involved in the death of Levi Bennett over ten years ago? Our viewers are probably wondering why things got so out of hand."

Vic listened without reacting until she finished speaking.

"First I'd like to say something. We agreed if I talked about that time in my life, I could make a statement to my family. They won't have anything to do with me," Vic said, causing Vivi to wince. "Hey, Mom," he said coldly.

Her mother cried softly on the phone. "I gave him so many chances. I tried to help him."

"I know, Mom." Vivi's heart broke for her mother.

"Okay, Mr. Clark. Say what you'd like to say," Connie told him.

Vic looked straight at the camera, the small smile now a full-on smirk. "Hey, Vivi."

Her stomach cramped. Oh, no. No, no, no. He was going to destroy her life. She just knew it.

"Honey, hang on tight," her mother whispered.

And Vic glanced at the interviewer. "Vivi's my sister," he explained, then looked back at the camera again, as if he were staring through her. "I heard you're an up-and-coming star at Club TEN29. Nice catch, baby sis."

Apparently the publicity train even reached behind bars, Vivi realized in horror. Too bad she hadn't thought about the ramifications of her performing at the guys' club when it came to her imprisoned brother's reaction. She'd considered him a nonissue. Oh, how wrong she'd been, and her stomach lurched at the prospect of what was to come.

"Look at you, playing in my backyard."

Vic's grin, she realized, was really a self-satisfied smirk. He'd always resented her. Hated how much her father adored her in comparison to how badly he'd treated Vic. And he'd never hesitated to punish her for it—when they were younger, hiding her toys, when they were older, planting demeaning rumors and whispers at school so the other kids would steer clear of her.

"You three, hiring my sister. I couldn't have planned it better myself, boys," he said as if he were speaking directly to Tanner, Jason ... and Landon. Clearly satisfied he'd done his damage, Vic leaned back in his chair and met the interviewer's gaze. "Now what did you want to talk about?" he asked nonchalantly.

Not wanting to hear any more, she turned off the television. "I hate him," she said to her mother, her throat full.

"I'm coming over." Her mom would drop everything to make sure Vivi was okay.

"No. I'll be fine. I have things I need to do today," she said, though Vic had just taken away her means of gently breaking the news to Landon. If he or his partners hadn't seen this broadcast, someone was bound to tell them about it.

Vivi knew how her brother thought. He might not know for a fact whether she'd informed the guys about her relationship to him, but it was a smart assumption that they wouldn't hire her if they'd known. But Vic could be certain this bombshell would destroy her life, and that had always been his goal.

Mission accomplished, she thought, all her hopes and dreams gone. She had no choice now but to face Landon and admit she'd omitted one very important fact without the ability to cushion the truth and explain her reasons.

They were going to be furious. They'd hate her by association. And they'd have every right to treat her badly. She was going to have to walk away from the opportunity of a lifetime, like she'd tried to do from the moment she'd made the connection between Vic and Landon. She only wished she'd tried harder. Then she wouldn't be in his predicament, and she wouldn't be falling for the club owner who probably couldn't stand the sight of her because she reminded him of losing his twin.

✧　✧　✧

LANDON HAD A long night. Once he'd gotten home from the club, he'd crashed hard, his dreams coming in alternate snippets, from hands and body all over Vivi to random appearances by his brother. Dreams of

80

Levi weren't new. He was often there, not speaking, lurking around but not a part of Landon's life in the dream. He would always wake up, pulse pounding, the pain in his heart a hole that would never be filled.

With a groan, he rose and took a long, hot shower and, when he came out, flipped on the television, made and poured himself a cup of coffee, and settled in to watch. He'd woken early, and he couldn't show up on Vivi's doorstep at the ass crack of dawn to talk about why she was running from him. So he needed to kill time.

He took a sip of his morning caffeine just as the announcer of the morning news show began to speak. "As you know, hazing has been in the news lately, as many college campuses are forced to reevaluate their policies regarding the issue of underage drinking on campus and in fraternities."

The subject caught his attention, and he grabbed the remote to raise the volume. She continued, naming the current universities who had had problems and sentences some of the kids involved had received. Stomach churning, he was about to change the channel when a familiar face came on the screen.

Vic. In what looked like a prison interview.

"What the fuck?" Landon paused mid-sip and placed the mug on the table.

He quickly shot off a joint text to Jason and Tanner to turn on the show, then focused on the screen.

"So, Mr. Clark, you're in prison for numerous crimes, but we're here to talk about hazing in particular."

The man looked the same as he had when he'd gone after Tanner recently, large and ripped, as if he'd had nothing to do in prison but work out. With the same self-righteous smirk he'd always had.

"I'd like to discuss your perspective. What was going through your mind at the time you were involved in the death of Levi Bennett over ten years ago? Our viewers are probably wondering why things got so out of hand."

"Son of a bitch." Landon's hands curled into fists. In the early days after Levi's death, they'd had plenty of requests for interviews, which they'd always declined. Nobody had called him about this. Apparently the families' feelings didn't mean jack shit.

"First I'd like to say something. We agreed if I talked about that time in my life, I could make a statement to my family. They won't have anything to do with me." Vic paused. "Hey, Mom," he said coldly.

"Okay, Mr. Clark. Say what you'd like to say."

Vic looked straight at the camera, that damned smirk bigger now. "Hey, Vivi."

Landon froze at the sound of the uncommon name, telling himself it was an ugly coincidence, but his heart beat like a jackhammer as he waited for the bastard to say more.

"Vivi's my sister," Vic said, looking at the camera. "I heard you're an up-and-coming star at Club TEN29. Nice catch, baby sis."

Landon froze.

"Look at you, playing in my backyard." Vic looked right at the television screen. "You three, hiring my sister. I couldn't have planned it better myself, boys." He leaned back in his chair and met the interviewer's gaze. "Now what did you want to talk about?" he asked as if he didn't have a care in the world.

Landon's cell phone began to ring, but his stomach was churning and his head was pounding, the shock of Vic's words and the truth about the woman he couldn't get out of his system reverberating in his head.

When he didn't answer the phone, it began to ring again. Instead of dealing with his friends, he picked up a glass bowl his mother had given him and threw it against the wall, but the crash and shattering sound didn't give him any satisfaction. Vivi, the woman he wanted with a fierceness he'd never experienced before, the woman who'd compelled him to play the piano again for the first time since his twin's passing over a decade ago, who he'd opened up to, was Victor Clark's sister. The man who'd killed his twin.

83

He couldn't stomach alcohol or he'd start drinking right now. So he trashed his apartment instead, kicking over his coffee table, breaking photograph frames on bookshelves, waiting for something to finally make him feel better. And when that didn't happen, he sunk down against a wall and wondered why fate wanted to fuck with him so badly.

He wasn't sure how much time had passed before the banging sounded on his door. Before he could decide whether he planned on answering, Tanner let himself in. Both he and Jason had keys to Landon's and vice versa in case of emergency.

"Shit, man. I came as fast as I could. Apparently not soon enough," Tanner said, his gaze taking in the destruction.

He strode into the room and headed over to one particular pile and began picking up the pictures. "Your mom's going to be pissed, you know. She's going to have to reframe all these." He set the broken frame on the sofa because the coffee table was upside down.

From his position on the floor, Landon looked up at his friend. "You're the one who couldn't look at Vic or utter his name without ending up behind bars. Why are you so fucking calm? He was taunting us." And that was the least of why Landon was so pissed off.

Tanner shook his head. "I'm not fucking calm, and

if I hadn't been with Scarlett when the interview came on, my place would look just like yours. That said, I've had years of therapy and now Scarlett in my life to show me what's important. I'm not going to let Vic destroy me." He paused. "Which is not to say I'm not pissed as hell we hired his sister." The muscle ticking in Tanner's jaw spoke to his anger.

He strode over and held out a hand, pulling Landon to his feet. "You have every reason to lose your shit. Now talk to me."

Landon ran a hand over his face and groaned. "Yesterday I was kissing her. That bastard's sister. Now I want nothing to do with her." But he couldn't forget her taste. The sweetness of her tongue rubbing against his, her warm, lush body grinding into his groin. Or the way she looked at him in compassionate understanding when he told her it felt wrong to play music when Levi couldn't. He'd bared his soul.

Lies. All fucking lies.

"Well, at least now I know why she's been pulling away." He kicked at a pile of pillows on the floor. "But it didn't stop her from signing the fucking contract," he muttered.

A knock sounded on the door, the lock disengaged, and this time Jason let himself in. "Jesus," the other man muttered, taking in the mess.

"I want her out of the club," Tanner said as Jason

joined them, stepping past glass and around the overturned cocktail table.

"So do I," Landon said, shoving his hands into his back jeans pockets.

"If she has half a heart, she'll walk away on her own," Tanner muttered.

Jason stepped up to both men, a serious expression on his face. "Nobody's breaking a contract, not us and not her. Regardless of how we feel personally, we have invested a shit ton of money into her summer promotion. We hired one of the most expensive companies in town, and tickets are sold based on her viral performance. Not to mention, she opens on Friday." Always the voice of reason, Jason stated a valid case.

"Dammit," Tanner muttered.

"Fuck." If Landon hadn't already destroyed the living room in his apartment, he'd do it now. "You're telling me I'm stuck with her for the summer."

"I'm telling you again, nobody's breaking this contract. Not us and not Vivi. If she wants out, I'll be more than happy to tell her tough shit and shove our ironclad contract down her throat," Jason said in a no-argument voice.

"Fine." Landon didn't like it, but he understood business and his partner was right. "But I don't want to deal with her."

Jason and Tanner exchanged glances. Yes, they'd all experienced the same horrific night and lost their friend. But Landon had lost his twin.

"Done. We'll work with Vivi," Jason said.

Tanner nodded. "Keep your distance. We'll handle things." He strode over to the coffee table. "Now let's get this place cleaned up."

Not for the first time, Landon thanked his blessings for having these men in his life.

THE DAY OF Vivi's brother's interview, she'd tried to reach Landon, but he hadn't answered his phone or replied to her texts. It hurt but she understood. First he'd probably been in shock, and once he'd come to his senses, he'd realized he'd been lusting after the enemies' sister. No doubt he'd assume she'd known all along and taken the job anyway. Which was partially true. It just didn't explain her reasons. Being stuck with her own thoughts all day had been painful, but she'd even turned Ellie away, needing to think.

Close to evening, she pulled on her big-girl panties and headed down to the club to see if any of the guys were present. She was nervous about who she'd find there. After what Vic had done to Landon's twin and to Tanner a few months ago, she sensed Jason would be the kindest of the three.

Her stomach churned when she saw Landon behind the bar, but she wasn't going to cower. She had to face this situation head on. Vic might have outed her, but she'd been the one to keep the information to herself. Now she had to face the music.

She walked over and placed her hands on the countertop. "Hi," she said, calling for his attention.

He turned from where he'd been looking toward the liquor bottles, staring at them for too long to be doing anything purposeful.

His hair was messed, as if he'd been running his hands through the soft strands, and visible tension and hurt etched his features. She hated that she was part of that pain.

"Something I can do for you?" he clipped out.

She swallowed hard at his cold tone. "I ... I wanted to talk to you. You didn't answer your phone or texts."

"I'm sure you can figure out why." He lifted a bar rag and began to rub down what appeared to be an already clean counter.

"Landon, when you first approached me with the job offer, I had no idea who you were. I don't speak to Vic. We're ... estranged."

"So he stated on national television. At least that's one point in your favor," he muttered.

She pulled herself onto a barstool. Obviously he

wasn't going to engage in meaningful conversation, and it was her job to explain, anyway. "After the offer came in for this opportunity, I went to your club's website. That's how I made the connection. I didn't know until then. And after I did, if you'll recall, I said no. I turned you down."

He stilled. "But you didn't say why."

She shook her head, and a part of her still didn't regret it. Now she had to make him understand why. "I didn't want to rub salt in an old and still-open wound. I mean, it didn't make sense to bring up Vic's name, to make you think about your twin's death. I didn't want to do that to you."

"I always think about Levi," he bit out. "It's there, every waking minute."

"And that's why I didn't say anything! It was kinder to say no and walk away, but you didn't let me."

"I remember," he said, leaning a hip on the bar. "So what changed your mind? The money? The prestige? The opportunities that would come from performing here for the summer?" he pressed, obviously certain she was mercenary at her core.

She squirmed in her seat because she'd be lying if she said all those things hadn't been appealing. "Okay, yes, those opportunities were attractive, of course, but you also explained that you'd all been through hell this past year, that the club took a downturn after some problems–"

"After your brother targeted us," he reminded her coldly.

She shivered, wrapping her arms around herself. "Yes. And then you insisted that my performing would help you rebuild. Get the people back into the club. And I thought, if you were right, I could help repay what my brother took from you. It was … it was a win-win."

Landon narrowed his gaze, still assessing her. "At least you're honest that you wanted to benefit, too. As for whether or not you gave a shit about helping us?" He shrugged. "Jury's out. I have no way of knowing."

Her heart twisted as she realized there was no getting through to him, and she raised her hands, giving up. "I'll go, okay? I'll pack up my things and be out of here tonight. My brother's done enough to hurt you. All of you. I don't want to stay here as a reminder and make things worse." She jumped up from her seat and turned to go.

"You can't leave, Vivi. We have an ironclad contract. You're obligated to stay and perform for the duration."

His words shocked her and she pivoted, narrowing her gaze. "Why? You don't like me, you don't trust me, and I know you want me far away from you and your friends. So why not let me out of my contract?"

"Because we've invested heavily in you and we've sold tickets based on your performance. Another entertainer won't do. Especially since you open Friday night. So go practice, because we may not like it, but you're our star act. We've paid and bought you, Vivi. Suck it up because *I* have to."

"Fuck you, Landon." She straightened her shoulders and faced him. She wasn't going to cower in front of any man, including the one her brother had tried to destroy.

"You may not like me, but you're right. We do have a contract, and I'm going to bring money and people to this club. And for the record, I'm not Vic. I'm nothing like my brother. So don't you dare talk to me like I'm something you scraped off your shoe." Gathering every ounce of self-respect she possessed, she spun around and stormed away.

Chapter Five

IN THE FEW days leading up to opening night, Landon struggled within himself. He was torn between what he should feel about Vivi and what he actually felt. He ought to be angry at her for keeping her identity a secret, but a part of him understood her reasons. He even appreciated her looking out for him, and yeah, he believed her when she said she hadn't wanted to cause him any more pain. Because in reality, she could have taken the job easily from the get-go, but she'd turned him down because she'd realized Landon's connection to her brother. So he trusted that she wasn't playing him.

He should be steering clear of her because of her blood relation to Vic, knowing that Levi's death would always be between them. And yet the more time that passed, the more he realized he was doing it because the guys thought he should. Not because he held a grudge against *her*.

Opening night, meanwhile, was coming together perfectly. The place would be packed, excitement in the air. The only thing that concerned him was Vivi's performance. She was solid in her practice, but the emotional component that usually drew him into her music was missing. It was as if with Vic's revelation and the change in how he and the guys treated her, she wasn't the same bubbly performer he'd grown used to seeing.

Watching her lack of sparkle, he realized she was suffering as much as he was, and if he didn't do something about it, opening night would be a bust, and he'd have only himself to blame.

So go practice, because we may not like it, but you're our star act. We've paid and bought you, Vivi. Suck it up because I have to. That had been a dick thing to say, and he'd regretted it the moment it came out of his mouth.

Seeing her pretty gaze dull had hit him in the gut. Despite his own pain, she was right. She wasn't her brother. She was a performer with heart, and right now hers was hurting. At the very least, she needed people in her corner tonight, and the club owners who'd hired her freezing her out was not going to make for a successful event.

So what was he going to do about it?

✧   ✧   ✧

VIVI BOUNCED AROUND the dressing room behind the stage, Ellie by her side, trying to keep her calm in the face of Owen reminding her of everything riding on this one performance.

"Remember, it's the start of something big, Vivienne. You never know who is going to be in the audience watching you. Be the star I know you are."

Ellie narrowed her gaze. "You're making her nervous," she finally snapped. "Do you see how antsy she is? Go away and let me calm her down."

With a frown, Owen walked out, leaving Vivi alone with her best friend.

"Are you okay?" Ellie asked, her brown eyes focused on Vivi with concern.

Vivi shook her hands out in front of her. "These past few days have been a challenge. Singing in front of Landon, knowing how much I hurt him… He's really been cold. Shutting me out."

They'd connected from the first time their eyes met, and it pained her to know she'd been the one to break things between them. "It's hard to perform when you feel the chill in the room."

"Come here. Let me give you a hug." Ellie put her arms around her and squeezed tight. "Now remember, and I'll deny it if you repeat it, but Owen's right. You're a star. Now go out there and show Landon what he's missing."

Vivi stepped back and sighed. "That's not it, Ellie. Even if he were able to forgive me, I'm not sure I could get over it myself. Knowing what my own brother did to him? To his family? Oh my God. There's no way we can get past this. I just need to do what Owen said. Impress someone big and wind up with a good gig that takes me far away from Landon Bennett."

Ellie frowned. "Let's not worry about anything except tonight, okay?"

"Okay. Now would you give me a few minutes alone? Let the guys in the band know I'm almost ready, and let's make some music."

ELECTRIC ENERGY VIBRATED in the packed-to-capacity club, and despite everything that had gone down with Vic, Landon and his partners were excited for Vivi's opening night. Faith accompanied Jason, Scarlett was with Tanner, and Landon sat beside them, but for all purposes, he was alone waiting for the entertainment to begin.

His foot tapped nervously against the floor, his anticipation for the evening high. He wanted nothing more than for Vivi to succeed, not just for the club but for her own benefit as well.

"Landon, how are you?" Scarlett asked, leaving Tanner's side to talk to him. "I heard you had a shock about Vivi. Tanner was upset, too. Is there anything I can do?"

"I'm fine," he assured her.

She clasped his hand. "You know that my brother died and the guys who killed him got off on a technicality."

He nodded. It'd been part of what kept her and Tanner apart for a while. Scarlett's need for justice and the fact that Tanner's arrest record for assault when he was younger had been expunged. "But Vivi didn't do anything wrong."

A pleased smile lit Scarlett's face. "Exactly what I reminded Tanner of when he went on a tirade about her the other night."

Landon shook his head. These women liked to meddle in the lives of people they cared about, and by virtue of his relationships with the men, Landon had become one of those people. He understood Scarlett was trying to tell him she approved of any relationship he might choose to have with Vivi. Tanner's opinion was still open to debate, along with Jason's.

Landon and his partners hadn't had a discussion about Vic or Vivi since the day in Landon's apartment after they'd discovered the truth. They'd had opposite shifts at the club, and truth be told, Landon had avoided his friends, not wanting them to know his feelings about Vivi and the fact she was related to Vic were changing. His hatred of Victor Clark would never go away. He didn't need to forgive the man to find peace. That notion was for other people, not him. Vic had no remorse, and for that reason, Landon would never forgive him. But Vivi? She was right. She wasn't her brother.

Jason and Tanner wouldn't understand that. They had no emotional connection to Vivi. Landon did. With a groan, he let his thoughts go. He'd deal with his friends when the time was right, but for now they needed to focus on making this night a success.

At that moment, Vivi's accompanying band started to play, and the loud talking around him turned into soft murmuring as all eyes turned to the stage. The large wall screen lit up in multicolored flashing lights that caused the crowd to go wild as the drummer built up in volume.

Suddenly the screen went black.

The music stopped.

Unexpected silence descended.

And before the audience could react, the screen flashed again, this time with colorful starbursts, and Vivi's voice sounded just as the lights went on above the stage. She stepped out to a loud cheer, wearing a sparkling red and black sequined bodysuit with cleavage-revealing cutouts on her chest, a black belt around her waist, and matching knee-high boots. Her makeup was heavier than he'd ever seen it, eyes surrounded by thick black liner and lashes, her lips a siren red.

At the sight of her, his heart nearly stopped and his cock hardened in his pants. A combination of need and pride centered in his chest. And then the patrons in the club erupted, joining with her cover songs. But he knew she had her own music to share, and that would blow the crowd away even more.

She'd engaged Landon from the second she stepped on stage, captivated him with her incredible voice, and her body movements had him imagining doing all sorts of dirty, sexy things both to her and with her. Hell, half the guys in this club were probably envisioning the same thing even if they'd walked in with dates.

Landon shifted in his seat, not so discreetly adjusting his dick because he was fucking uncomfortable. But he couldn't deny how much he enjoyed her performance. He glanced at his partners and noticed their women wrapped around them but huge smiles on their faces. No doubt they were counting the money they'd bring in when word of mouth took hold about tonight.

From his seat by the bar, Jason raised his bottle of Pellegrino and grinned. Tanner caught the gesture and did the same, Landon joining them. Club TEN29 was back and they had Vivi to thank.

The rest of the night went off without a hitch, her

songs and acts all perfection. Her varied costume changes drove him insane. Bodysuits that showed off her legs, ones with skintight shorts attached, sparkles, sequins, fishnet stockings, thigh-high boots, high heels, ballet slippers, all designed to make a man drool. To make *him* drool.

And the pull toward her wasn't just sexual. There was a vulnerability buried inside her that allowed her music to shine and her sensuality to burn. He felt those things deep inside him, and as she sat down at the piano, slowing down her final set, the sound of the keys playing called to him.

Unable to stop himself, he made his way toward the stage, where she played the instrument he loved. As if she sensed his presence, she looked up, her gaze locked with his, and the rest of the room dissolved around them. He made his way to the bench and settled in beside her. Their shoulders rubbed against each other, the warmth of her body penetrating through his jacket, and the vocals she projected reverberated inside him. Even if it was just his imagination, she helped piece together the jagged parts inside him.

Without words, he watched as her fingers traveled the keyboard, taking the song down an octave, leaving room for him to play along with her. His mouth grew dry and he began to sweat, the thought of playing in public fucking frightening. Music always reminded him of Levi.

But that could be a good thing, he thought, his fingers touching the keys. He loved his twin. Missed him, yes, but reminders could be cathartic. So he began to play for just the second time in a decade, while her beautiful voice resonated around him.

She laid her head on his shoulder as she sang the slow, moving song about love and loss. And then she lifted her head, turned, and met his gaze, her smile as brilliant as the applause was deafening. She rose to take a bow and, he knew, step back on the stage for her closing number.

He sat alone on the bench, stunned by the emotions flowing through him, as if something inside him had been set free by that performance. He owed the flow of emotion and the ultimate acceptance of that part of him he'd lost with Levi's death to Vivi.

He desired her. He needed her. His body yearned to feel her beneath him. The rest, the hard parts, the fact that they had an upward climb toward any kind of relationship, he'd have to deal with later. He was willing to fight through the hurdles of his friends and family to get to know her completely.

He didn't know what the future held, but he couldn't hold her brother's sins against her.

✧　✧　✧

ELATION SOARED THROUGH Vivi at the close of her first event at the club. The excitement of a job well done was as much a reason for her heightened emotions as the fact that Landon had sat with her at the piano. Surely he wouldn't have done it if he still held a grudge. She'd sensed his initial reluctance to play, but he'd joined her and together they'd made magic. She knew he sensed it, too.

Her desire for him was real, but so was the knowledge that nothing could come of it ... for so many reasons. Pushing those negative thoughts aside, she'd taken her bows, performed an encore, and now stood in her dressing room, flowers from her mom on her makeup counter. Her mom and Ellie were chatting on one side of her, and Owen was taking bows and congratulations from people coming backstage, as if he'd been the one to succeed.

So far none of the club owners had come to see her, Landon included, and she tried not to let her disappointment dampen her spirits about an otherwise fabulous night.

"I'm so proud of you," her mother said, pulling her into a hug. "I cannot believe that was my baby girl up on that stage."

Vivi grinned. "Thanks."

"You and I needed something wonderful this week," her mom said. "Thank you for providing it. Now if you two don't mind, I'll get going."

Ellie glanced at her. "Can I share a ride? I'm on your way," she said.

"Of course."

Vivi hugged them both goodbye. "Thanks for your support. Love you both."

"Love you, too." Her mother waved and Ellie did the same before they headed out.

"Vivienne, can I talk to you?" Owen waved her over, and she joined him, noticing he was talking to a good-looking man in a pair of black jeans and a sport jacket. His pale blond hair was carefully styled, and his high cheekbones and chiseled features definitely spoke of his Nordic heritage.

"Vivienne, this is Axel Matsen, a—"

"Promoter! Oh my God, I know your name." Axel had put many a pop star on the map. "It's so nice to meet you." She shook his hand, and when she began to pull back, he kept her palm against his.

"Fabulous performance, Vivienne," he said.

"Vivi. I go by Vivi Z as my stage name. Owen just has a thing for my full name." He thought it was elegant and gave her credibility, or some such nonsense.

He smiled and stepped into her personal space, her

hand still in his. "Well, Vivi Z, I have big ideas for you if you and your agent want to hear them."

Owen cleared his throat. "I'm sure the offers are going to come flying in," he said, just as Vivi spoke, too. "I'd be very interested in hearing what you have to say." She might not like his mannerisms, but she understood how important he was in the business.

She glanced down at their intertwined hands, uncomfortable with both how close he stood and the fact that he hadn't let her go. No matter how much she wanted more from singing, she wasn't going to let any man take advantage of her, and this was just his initial step. With a hard wrench of her wrist, she finally managed to twist her hand away.

He grinned, his leering gaze on hers. "Good to know. I'll be in touch with your agent and perhaps we can get together for lunch. You're going places," he assured her.

Her stomach twisted in a mixture of pleasure, excitement, and nerves.

"She has a contract through the end of the summer," a familiar voice said from behind her in a firm ... and arousing tone. Landon stepped up beside Vivi.

"Landon Bennett, owner of this club." He extended his hand, and if she wasn't mistaken, he and Axel had a pissing contest over their firm handshake before each man released his grip.

"She's yours … for now," Axel said and, without sparing Landon another glance, looked to Owen. "I'll be in touch," he said. "Vivi, it was a pleasure."

He walked away and Landon immediately glared at Owen. "When she's with you, she's your responsibility. I saw her trying to extricate herself from his grip from across the room. If you're going to let slimy promoters hang on to her hand too long, who's to say you won't let them push her for other things?"

Vivi blinked in shock at his protective accusations because he was right. Owen hadn't stepped in to help. Though she'd freed herself from Axel's grip, she needed to be more aware and not put herself in positions where she was alone with people who made her uncomfortable.

"If you can't handle the job of protecting your client, she should find someone who can," Landon said, stepping into Owen's space.

"You're right," he said, holding up his hands in surrender. "That was my mistake. I'll be more careful in the future."

"Okay, I can take care of myself, both of you. Landon, I appreciate you looking out for me. Owen, yes, just be more aware. Now can we move on?"

Owen inclined his head. "I'll be going. Just a reminder, I'll be vetting offers throughout the week.

Good job, Vivienne."

She smiled, and as he walked out, she realized she was alone with Landon, a man she truly desired but didn't think she had a chance of ever having. But if given the opportunity, she'd make the most of every second they had together, knowing whatever they shared could never last.

LANDON HAD HEARD that asshole Axel tell Vivi she was going places right after he'd watched him invade her personal space and seen an uncomfortable look cross her face. He hadn't been able to get across the room fast enough to rip the man's hand out of hers. And her damned agent needed a kick in the ass to make him pay attention to what was going on around him. The woman was going to end up needing protection from the people around her, he thought, shocked with how deeply he wanted to be the person who was there for her.

She drew a deep breath and faced him, her expression wary. Obviously she didn't know what he was thinking when it came to her and he didn't blame her. He'd been an asshole last time they'd been alone.

"So … tonight was unexpected," she said, her face still flushed from her performance.

"You can say that again." As if drawn by an invisible cord, he'd approached her … and found himself part of her act. He treated her to a wry grin. "Tonight was a shock but not as much as the first time I played along with you. And I have to admit, it gave me a sense of peace about Levi. Maybe for the first time."

She grasped his hand, and he curled his fingers around hers, finding comfort and a jolt of arousal at her touch. "I'm glad. It's what I was hoping for. Although I didn't expect you to join me with an audience."

He shrugged. "Like you said, it was an unexpected night."

He stared at her, lost as to what to say next. Finally he decided to break the ice with the what was probably on both of their minds. "Look, I don't like that you're related to Vic. It's the worst possible scenario." He held on tight to her hand. "But I know you tried your best to back out of this situation. I pushed you to take the job."

She swallowed hard, meeting his gaze with a vulnerable look in her eyes. "Vic is something that's always going to be between us. I get that. But if I can have your understanding, if you don't blame me for not telling you who I am, that's enough for me."

He paused, knowing now was the time to walk away if that's what he wanted … but in his heart he couldn't do it. "What if it's not enough for *me*?" he asked.

Sadness crossed her face. "We have too much to overcome for anything serious between us. Your friends, your family, and what my brother did. Not to mention, I might be leaving at the end of the summer, hopefully to go on tour with a big act."

His stomach clenched at the thought of her leaving but also with the truth of her words, yet he refused to let anything stand in the way of him having her. "Ever hear of one day at a time?"

He held out his arms and she ran, jumping into them and wrapping her long legs around his waist. Whatever time they had together, he'd take it and deal with the issues later, he thought, as their lips joined.

A few steps and he backed her against the wall, his mouth hard on hers, the kiss long overdue. Kissing her felt right, and he didn't plan to stop for a long time. His cock throbbed in his pants, pulsing against her soft heat as his mouth devoured hers.

They stood in place, her legs tight around him, the warmth of her sweet body pressing against him, his fingers gliding up and down her sides and over her breasts, which fit perfectly in his hands.

Her nipples puckered, tightening against his palms, but the slick bodysuit material kept him from feeling her supple flesh, and he needed skin-to-skin contact. "Upstairs," he said, breaking the kiss long enough to tell her what he needed.

"My bed." A sexy smile lifted her lips.

Obviously she was willing, at least for tonight, and he was happy to take whatever she offered.

She lowered her legs, and he waited until her feet hit the floor, steadying her before releasing his grasp.

They needed to walk through the bar to get to the elevator, and though he'd prefer a route that didn't involve passing by people who might stop them for conversation, he didn't care.

"Ready? Or do you need to get your things?" he asked.

She opened a drawer and pulled out her keys. "I'm good to go."

Knowing he was making a statement he'd have to deal with later, he grasped her free hand and led her out through the bar. His partners were with their women, and he caught Tanner's gaze, nodding his head and silently daring him to start trouble. He already knew how they felt about Vivi. The same way he'd felt only yesterday, except *he'd* been in denial.

He'd just have to deal with Tanner and Jason later. He led her to the elevator and stepped through the doors the second they opened. Although desire was a low, heavy pounding inside him and he wanted nothing more than to press her against the wall again, they'd be upstairs quickly and he'd have her in his arms soon enough.

Finally, the doors reopened and they walked into the hall. Fumbling with the keys, she let them into the apartment, and he kicked the door closed behind them, then she dropped the keys on a foyer shelf and spun to face him.

His heart beat heavily in his chest as he took in her shapely body and those well-kissed lips, and his cock gave a jerk of approval. "Undress," he said in a gruff voice. He knew better than to think he could get that tight material off her by himself.

She toed off her ballet slippers, then bit down on her lower lip, the tiny movement incredibly sexy. As he watched, she pulled at the rounded neck and slid one arm out of the stretchy material, then tugged again so she could free her other arm and expose her perfect breasts. No bra, her hard, perky nipples calling to him and causing his mouth to run dry.

He took half a step forward and she held out a hand.

"I'm not finished." And with that statement, she hooked her thumbs into the sides of her bodysuit and pulled it down, taking her lace stockings along with all that confining material.

She pushed it past her hips, then her thighs. And fuck him because she bent over and removed every-thing, kicking the clothing aside and standing before him gloriously naked. Her body was a sight to behold, small but perfect breasts, dusky tight nipples, and her pussy glistening, calling to him.

"Am I going to stand here naked by myself?" she asked in a teasing voice.

He grinned and let his sport jacket slide to the floor. She came to him, her nimble fingers quickly releasing his shirt buttons, pushing the material off his shoulders so it joined his jacket. She pressed her hands to his chest, her painted nails scraping over his nipples before her hands slid lower and she unhooked his pants and undid the zipper.

Before he could process her next move, she'd dipped her hand inside his boxer briefs and gripped his aching cock in her palm. "Mmm. Smooth. Hard. Is this all for me?"

"Every last inch." He kissed her hard on the lips, and she released his dick, working instead on lowering his pants to the floor so he could kick them aside. Then he pulled her flush against him, skin to skin at last.

Her perky nipples pressed into his chest and she moaned. "Now this is more like it," he muttered, savoring her warmth and the feel of her in his arms.

"How about a shower?" she asked.

He met her gaze.

"I just had a really long set and I could use one."

Her cheeks flushed an adorable pink at the request.

"Come." Knowing the layout of the apartment, he took her hand and led her into the bedroom and adjoining bath.

While she ran the water, he traced the length of her spine with his hand, then followed it with his lips, feeling her tremble, knowing he was arousing her with the slightest touch.

They stepped under the warm water, and when she turned in his arms, he blanked out in utter bliss. The heat of her body, the softness of her skin, the way she fit against him ... all perfect.

Breaking contact, he reached for the body wash, realizing he was going to smell like fruit when he was finished, but so would she. And he'd be the one who rubbed the suds over her creamy skin. He considered that a win.

He soaped up his hands and began a thorough cleaning, making sure he touched every inch of her flesh, from her pink-painted toes up over her legs, calves, knees, and thighs, pausing at the creases where her thighs met her pussy.

She gasped and grabbed his shoulders, holding on while he slid his fingers lightly over her sex, tracing his way around the delicate folds and landing on her clit.

"Landon," she murmured, arching onto her toes, trying to get him to press harder.

He had no problem complying. "Do you like that?"

Taking her sigh of pleasure as a *yes*, he circled his slippery finger over her clit, back and forth, until her fingers were digging into his shoulders and she was rocking her hips in time to his movement.

He felt the moment she climaxed, her body stiffening and a low moan coming from the back of her throat. Nothing was better than the sound of a satisfied woman, he thought, holding on to her as she came, then sweeping a kiss over her mouth.

She glanced up, her wet fringed lashes fluttering over her eyes as she blinked up at him, a pleasured smile lifting her lips. He brushed a kiss over her mouth before returning to their shower, which was a rush to get out and into bed. No way would he let her touch his cock or he'd go off like a firecracker, and he wanted to be inside her when he came the first time.

After she'd washed and conditioned her hair and he'd soaped up and done the same, they climbed out of the shower and wrapped themselves in white fluffy towels.

"Are you hungry?" he asked, knowing she probably hadn't had anything to eat since before the concert.

Darkened eyes met his. "I'm hungry for you."

✧   ✧   ✧

VIVI WRUNG OUT and dried her hair as best she could, the rest of her wrapped in a towel. Tanner let his towel drop and Vivi's gaze traveled over his olive-colored skin and defined muscles. Though her sex still quivered from her orgasm, she could have another one from just looking at his gorgeous body, she thought, pulling her bottom lip into her mouth, then releasing it.

His hot gaze meeting hers, he reached out and plucked at where she'd tucked in the towel, letting it fall. "Bed, Vivi."

When he was hot for her, he was a man of few words and she liked it.

She spun and headed for the other room, settling on the mattress just as he climbed on and covered her body with his. Closing her eyes, she wrapped her arms around him and moaned, his cock throbbing against her core. She parted her legs, and he settled deeper against her, bracing his hands on either side of her head and pushing himself up, meeting her gaze. "Condom?" he asked.

"Just a colored-packet joke pack Ellie got me for my birthday. It had been awhile, and she thought maybe it would encourage me to get back out there," she said with a grin.

He shook his head and laughed. "Not sure I can imagine myself in…"

"Blue."

"At least it's not pink. Where can I grab them?" he asked.

She tipped her head right. "Nightstand drawer." She hoped he wouldn't ask why she'd kept them when she moved. It had been an impulse and now she was glad she had.

He slid to the side and opened the drawer, returning with the colorful packet. "You didn't mention it was *neon* blue."

She shrugged. "Do you think your manliness can handle it?"

He pushed to a sitting position, grabbed his cock, and pumped his hand up and down the thick shaft. "Still worried?" he asked with a wink.

She laughed, grateful for the lightness between them. She knew this night was nothing more than fulfilling mutual need, and when he came to his senses, or his friends or family pushed hard enough, *she'd* be the casualty. But she'd told herself she'd take what she could get with him, and she meant to keep that promise.

He ripped the packet and rolled on the condom, which was bright and big on his heavy cock.

"Blue is your color," she said, giggling, but she stopped laughing when he rose over her and he was poised at her entrance.

"I want you, Vivi," he said, growing serious.

She swallowed hard. "I want you, too." So much. It was crazy how much she felt for this man who was totally off-limits to her in the long run.

He slid his hand between her thighs and slicked his finger over her sex, coating her with her own wetness, then pushed inside her. "You ready for me, beautiful?"

Her throat swelled at the compliment. "Yes."

He hooked his finger inside her, and she moaned as he pressed on the right spot to arouse her incredibly fast. He pumped his finger in and out until she was breathing fast and waves of arousal hit her without warning, a hard and quick climax overtaking her. Then, while she was still coming, he removed his finger and thrust, his hard cock settling deep inside. He filled her completely, and the ripples that had already begun picked up again as he began to thrust into her.

"Eyes open, Vivi. I want you to look at me."

But she didn't want that. Looking into his eyes while he took her would only bond them further, and she already felt too much for this man. But she did as he asked, keeping her gaze steady on his as he slid in and out, grinding his hips against her with every successive push.

She tightened her legs around his hips and arched up, meeting him thrust for thrust until waves of pleasure took hold once more.

"Oh. Oh. God." Another orgasm hit with more force than the first, his thick cock swelling inside her. "Landon, harder please."

He complied and she fell apart, glorious waves of satisfaction flowing through her.

When she relaxed against him, he pulled out and lifted her up. "On your knees."

She blinked, her body limp from coming so hard, but clearly he had other ideas for them. So she settled on her hands and knees. He wrapped himself around her, his cock nudging at her entrance. Hooking his arm around her belly, his other hand on her hip, he began to take her in a hard pounding rhythm. Just as she was convinced that she couldn't possibly come again, his cock hit the right spot and she saw stars. She pushed back against him, meeting him as he worked his way toward his own orgasm.

To her shock, his shout of pleasure triggered her own release, a third climax that, if it weren't for his arm securely around her, would have caused her to fall onto the bed.

"Vivi, fuck, you feel good." Her body trembled at his words.

Finally they both collapsed, his heaviness pressing her onto the bed and his big body feeling so good cushioning hers. *Don't get used to it*, a little voice told her. But for right now, his weight against her was everything she needed and wanted.

Chapter Six

LANDON FELL INTO a deep sleep, his body curled around Vivi's softer one. Though he normally had a fitful night, dreams of Levi always occupying his mind, this morning he woke up realizing he'd had his first solid eight hours in what felt like forever. He owed it to the woman in his arms. Something about her soothed him, which made no sense considering who Vivi's brother was, but Landon wasn't about to argue with facts.

He'd have enough people to argue with in his life soon enough. Leaning over, he kissed Vivi's soft lips and she moaned, her eyes fluttering open.

"Good morning," she murmured.

"Morning."

"What time is it?" she asked.

He lifted his arms and stretched, planning to scoop her up and make love to her again. "Almost nine."

"Oh my God! I have to be at the recording studio in half an hour." She scrambled out of bed, leaving him disappointed and stuck with an erection he had no outlet for.

"Hey," he called out.

Naked, which only served to strengthen his morning wood, he crooked a finger. "At least give me a better good-morning kiss."

With a sexy smile on her lips, she walked back to the bed and leaned over, sealing her lips over his. He grabbed her and yanked her on top of him, the comforter separating their bodies, but he didn't care. He had her in his arms.

"Landon, you do not play fair." Her bottom lip slid out in an adorable pout.

He nipped at her there. "Never said I did." He kissed her long and hard, then slapped her ass. "Now go or you'll be late." He could get into a long conversation about where things between them were headed but had already decided against it.

He'd promised her they'd take things one day at a time, and he'd keep his word. He just planned to be around each and every day until she realized things between them could, somehow, work out.

VIVI RUSHED THROUGH her shower, dressed, and was downstairs before Landon even climbed out of bed. She walked through the club, startled when she heard someone call her name.

She spun around to see Tanner leaning against the bar, an iPad in front of him.

"Can we talk for a minute?" he asked.

Of all the partners, Tanner was the most intimidating. A well-built man, he exuded less charm and more power, and an aloofness that made her uncomfortable. Knowing he'd seen her leave with Landon last night, she could only imagine what he had to say to her now.

"Sure." She strode over and slid onto a barstool, determined not to shrink under his serious gaze. "What's up?"

"So. You and Landon." Tanner leaned one arm against the shiny glass and wood.

She narrowed her gaze. "You don't strike me as a gossipy guy, so let's just cut to the chase." She dropped her bag to the floor, settling in. "You don't want me with your friend."

His eyes flashed with something akin to respect. "Normally, what my friend does with his love life isn't any of my business." He pushed the tablet he'd been looking at aside. "But you're Vic's sister and that changes everything. I would think you'd have enough smarts to back off on your own."

She swallowed hard. "Not that I owe you an explanation, but don't you think I tried? Landon's persistent when he wants something." And the chemistry and need between them couldn't be denied. Not

121

that she'd admit as much to Tanner. "And what you said applies. Landon and I are none of your business."

But the fact that his best friend didn't approve? As much as Vivi had expected it, it hurt.

"Look," he said. "I'm sure you're a nice woman. But you bring up all sorts of shitty memories. No offense."

She gritted her teeth. "None taken," she lied, accepting that she'd forever be tainted by her brother's actions. And it sucked. "Now if you're finished expressing your disapproval, I have a recording session to get to." Leaning down, she picked up her bag, then straightened, meeting Tanner's gaze.

A flash of regret flickered across his features. "None of us created this situation," he said in a softer voice.

"Except my brother. I. Know." She hefted her bag over her shoulder and walked away, head and heart hurting.

Vivi spent the rest of the day with people she loved, she and her band finally getting an opportunity to record their music. Together they created magic, and she was extremely happy with the way things were coming together for her professionally.

On a personal level, her body still hummed from her time with Landon. He'd been a thorough lover, showing her all she'd been missing with other men. He played her body as well as he played the piano, pressing all the right keys to make her sing beneath his hands. Alone, just the two of them, things were perfect. Unfortunately life wasn't about two people living in a bubble. And though she'd tried to put Tanner's words out of her mind, whenever she took a break, his disapproval returned, ruining what happiness and satisfaction she found in her work and with Landon.

Two things she'd come to realize after today. If nothing else came of this summer at Club Ten29, she'd leave with a full set of recordings for big labels to consider, and if she wasn't careful, she'd also end up with a broken heart.

LANDON STEPPED OUT of the elevator in time to see Vivi grab her bag and rush away from Tanner, and a knot formed in his stomach. Heading over to the bar, he slammed a hand onto the counter to catch his friend's attention.

"Hey. Did you say something to upset her?" Landon gestured to the door that Vivi had walked out of.

"Looks like I'm getting no work done this morning," Tanner said with a groan and pushed aside the iPad he'd been looking at. "I didn't say anything other than the truth."

"Which is?" Landon pulled up a stool and sat down, leaning an arm on the counter.

Obviously resigned to a conversation, Tanner grabbed two bottles of water out of the fridge, sliding one across the counter to Landon. "That she's Vic's sister and she comes with bad memories and baggage." Opening the cap, he took a long sip, not meeting Landon's gaze.

"What else?" Because Landon knew his friend inside and out, and the man wasn't being one hundred percent honest.

Tanner clenched and unclenched his jaw. "I might have mentioned that if she were smart she'd back off on her own. Fuck, man, you can do better than that bastard's sister."

Hands curling into fists at his sides, Landon glared. "Did I tell you to stay away from Scarlett? That a DA had no place in the life of someone once arrested for assault? Or did I back you the fuck up when you wanted to run?"

Tanner shook his head. "It's not the same thing."

"No, it isn't. In that case, you were the one who'd done something shitty. But Vivi wasn't in that basement. She didn't kill my brother." He paused and drew a deep breath. "And she doesn't have a relationship with the man who did. She isn't making excuses for him. Hell, she doesn't even want anything to do with

Vic." Defending Vivi seemed right to him, a necessity or else he'd lose something precious.

Tanner frowned. "But—"

"No buts. Either you're on my side or you aren't. I'm not walking away from her, so make your choice." Landon's breath came out in harsh rasps as he went up against one of the men who'd saved him from losing his mind at a fragile time in his life.

His friend lowered his head for a moment before looking up. "I'm looking out for you. She's Vic's sister!"

"But she's not Vic!" Landon yelled back. "If Jason or I disapproved of Scarlett, would you have walked away?"

With a groan, Tanner shook his head and leaned against the bar. "But you just met her and... Fuck." His voice trailed off as his memory of his time with Scarlett obviously kicked in.

He'd laid eyes on her at the bar, taken her upstairs, and hadn't wanted to let her go. Too bad for him, she'd taken off when he got called away on business, but luckily she'd left a bracelet in his bed and returned for it later the next day.

"Jason reacted the same way when he ran into Faith. Hell, he moved her in with him almost immediately when she was in danger. He knew quickly. So did you."

"Shit. I made her feel bad." Tanner slammed his hand down on the counter, his guilty expression enough for Landon to forgive him.

He still winced, imagining how badly Vivi had taken the fact that one of his best friend's didn't want her in his life. She probably assumed Jason felt the same way. And Landon wasn't sure that Jason also didn't want Vic's sister in Landon's life, which meant he'd have to have a similar discussion with his other partner.

Speaking of Jason... "If I remember correctly, Tanner, you were rough on Faith, too." Landon recalled the time when Jason had brought Faith to the club so she wasn't left alone and Tanner had been a dick. "Look, I know you worry for the people you care about, but sometimes you have to trust that we know what's best for ourselves."

Of them all, Tanner had the roughest life growing up. His father had been an abusive bastard, and Tanner had learned to protect the people he cared about by fighting. It had taken being arrested and Jason pulling strings to get his record expunged for Tanner to get his head on straight. These days his punches were in the gym only. But old protective habits died hard, and Landon understood that Vivi's relation to Vic was a tough pill to swallow.

It wasn't that it was easy for Landon, it was more

that she'd gotten to him in a way that no woman ever had, enough that he was willing to deal with whatever baggage came along with her. That said, he didn't know if he'd feel the same way if she and her brother were close. Thankfully that wasn't something he needed to worry about.

"I'm sorry, man. I'll try and see her for who she is and not who she's related to." Tanner raised his water bottle and took a sip.

"That's all I can ask." Landon blew out a long breath, wondering how much damage Tanner's well-meaning but no doubt asshole-ish words had done.

Vivi already thought they were doomed from the start. He'd have an uphill road convincing her to do what Tanner had said, to see herself for who she was and not as Vic's sister, especially when it came to having a relationship with him.

His cell rang, drawing his attention from their conversation. He glanced down to see his father's name. He'd spoken to his parents once since the interview had broken. Apparently the news station had asked them for an interview as well but they'd turned down the request. They'd been upset enough about Victor discussing Levi's death on national television so many years later. Landon hadn't thought it was the right time to tell them he was in a relationship with the man's sister. That was something that had to be done in person. Explained face-to-face.

They needed to meet Vivi and see what he did, a sweet, warm, giving woman who'd distanced herself from her brother.

KNOWING BETTER BUT unable to help herself, Vivi read the online reviews for her performance last night while in an Uber on her way back from the recording studio. Her stomach was in knots as she opened her phone and pulled up Owen's email with the links.

A star is born.
Exceptional talent.
Brainy, beautiful, and going places.

Most of the reviews noted that the songs she'd written herself had the most depth and brought the most credibility to her voice. Tears filled her eyes in both awe and gratitude.

How many years had she lain in bed at night, dreaming of performing on a stage in front of people? Of having her songs reach the masses? Of one day becoming a household name?

She was lucky enough to have her songs reaching people now, to be able to spend days recording, and she knew she was bringing people into Club TEN29. At the very least, she was paying forward what they'd given to her. She wasn't going to dwell on Vic or be able to make up for what he'd done.

Tanner had made it clear how he felt, and she had no doubt Jason agreed with him. It didn't matter whether or not they liked her or cared if she was in a relationship with Landon, because she wasn't here forever. Her dreams were bigger and she finally saw a way to accomplish them, ironically, courtesy of Tanner and his friends.

The rest of the weekend passed quickly. Her Saturday and Sunday night performances were even better than her first, and she wasn't being modest. Owen brought in producers to talk to her and promoters. Suddenly she was a hot commodity, and she didn't have time after her shows to worry about Tanner's or Jason's feelings. She was, however, aware of Landon. Even as she met with industry people, she felt the heat of his gaze on her the entire time.

Just as with Axel, she knew he was watching over her, making sure everyone treated her with the utmost respect, or he was the one coming over to the table with drinks to make sure she was okay. He never had to say a word. It was obvious by his tone and demeanor he'd staked his claim. But he respected her space and her business and he didn't intrude. In fact, other than a wink when no one else was looking, he kept his distance while she worked. He didn't even give an encore with her at the piano, and at the end of each long night, she went upstairs alone.

Which was why she was shocked when a knock sounded at her door Monday morning. She had the day off, both from recording and performing, and she'd planned to stay in all day and relax.

She opened the door to find Landon wearing a pair of navy boarding shorts, a light blue tee shirt, and a sexy smile on his face.

"Hi."

"Morning."

"Umm, what are you doing here?" she asked.

"Pool day."

She narrowed her gaze. "What?"

"I'm here to take you swimming, so why don't you change, I'll wait, and we can get going." He leaned a hand on the doorframe, watching her expectantly.

The last thing she'd expected was a day outdoors. "Where do you plan to take me?"

He tapped her nose and grinned. "That's a surprise. Do you have other plans?"

She immediately shook her head, though if she'd been smart, she'd have hesitated. Since the night she'd been with him, she'd managed to keep her distance, and she'd thought, despite his watchful behavior, he'd decided to do the same. Though she'd been disappointed as the two days passed and he hadn't tried to come upstairs with her again, she understood he'd probably come to his senses. Or that Tanner had gotten through to him in some way, and she'd convinced herself it was for the best.

He stepped inside and shut the door behind them. "Then go put on a bathing suit and let's get going."

"Okay." The word was out before she could think. Again.

So she headed for the bedroom and changed into the bikini she owned but rarely had time to wear. She grabbed an extra-long tee shirt to cover the bathing suit, a pair of flip-flops in her hand, and packed a light bag as if she were going to the beach, including change of clothes, sunglasses, and her phone.

"I'm ready," she said, walking out and joining him in the outer room and tossing her things onto the sofa.

His gaze settled on her body and seared her skin, his eyes darkening as he took her in. "Put that tee shirt on or we're not going to make it to the pool."

Her nipples puckered beneath his heated gaze and her sex pulsed with desire, but she also wanted to know what he had planned. "Fine." She pulled the tee shirt over her head, let the hem fall to mid-thigh, and slipped on her flip-flops. "Ready."

He grinned and held out his hand, waiting until she slid her palm against his before clasping his fingers around her. "Let's get out of here."

131

After taking the elevator down, they walked through the club and she caught sight of Tanner at the bar.

"Vivi, come here, please?" Tanner called from across the room.

She glanced at Landon and he paused mid-stride. "It's up to you if you want to hear him out."

He was her boss, so... "Sure." She released his grasp and headed over to where the other man sat waiting. She didn't know what he wanted but assumed he'd be on his best behavior in front of Landon.

"I owe you an apology," he said before she could speak, taking her by utter surprise.

"Oh. I–"

"I was out of line the other day. The things I said to you were hypocritical. Something Landon pointed out to me." He propped a hip against the bar. "You see, when I met Scarlett, that was it for me. Nobody could have kept me away from her. So it's not my place to tell anyone what to do. Not to mention, I'm not a Boy Scout myself. I'm not Vic but I've done some shitty things. Let's just say I won't be giving you a hard time again."

"Umm, wow. Thank you. I appreciate that. And Jason?"

"Are you kidding? He found Faith on the side of the road with a flat tire and moved her in within a week. He won't have anything to say."

She shook her head. "We're not like that." She needed to clarify her relationship with Landon so nobody misunderstood, including Landon. "According to my agent, there should be some big offers coming through by the end of the summer. Things I've dreamed about since I was a kid." She glanced up at Landon, her heart pounding as she spoke, a shocking feeling of disappointment running through her at the thought of leaving him. "I'm sure it will involve a lot of travel."

A flash of dismay flickered across his face but he masked it quickly. "But we aren't going to worry about the future now. We're off to the pool." He tugged on her hand, and she told herself to put her thoughts aside and to just enjoy the time she had now.

Landon looked at his friend. "Thanks," he said, leading her out the door and to his SUV parked behind the club.

The sun was hot overhead, the warmth of the summer beating down on them. A perfect beach day, she thought, but he'd said they were going to a pool.

"So … where is this pool?" she asked again.

He rolled his eyes. "I take it you weren't good with surprises as a kid?" he asked as he opened her door and she climbed in.

He shut it behind her and entered the SUV on the

driver's side. Suddenly she was in an enclosed space with a man who smelled delicious and who she wanted desperately. Shifting in her seat, she turned toward him. "No, I used to shake my Christmas gifts under the tree."

He laughed. "Naughty girl," he said in a joking voice.

She slipped her shoes off and curled her legs beneath her on the seat. "I can be. Under the right circumstances," she teased right back.

He glanced over and she fluttered her eyelashes at him and grinned.

LANDON PULLED UP to his parents' house, knowing they were away for the weekend. He had the key and permission to use the pool during the summertime, so he'd decided to bring Vivi here for some alone time and a swim. She'd worked hard all weekend and had been bombarded with people wanting her attention, and here she could relax and not worry about anything but the sun ... and hopefully him.

"Where are we?" she asked as he cut the engine, placed an arm on the steering wheel, and turned to face her.

"We are at Casa Bennett. My parents have a pool."

Her face grew pale and her eyes went wide. "Your

parents? Oh, no. I can't meet them. I'm Vic's sister. My brother killed—" She slammed her jaw shut and looked out the window. "You *know*," she said. "How could you bring me here?"

He slid a hand onto her shoulder and brushed her hair away. "Hey. They're away, okay? Relax." He hadn't meant to throw her off-balance.

Her shoulders eased down and he realized she was shaking. He squeezed with one hand, trying to calm her. "Jesus. I'm sorry, Vivi. It wasn't such a good surprise after all." Sure, he'd thought about her meeting his parents and knew he had to break the news to them first.

She tipped her head and looked up at him. "This is why we're a bad idea."

Ignoring her statement, he leaned in and pressed his lips to hers. Sparks flew immediately, desire arcing between them so fast and furious her mouth opened beneath his. His tongue glided against hers and she moaned, their mouths joining, feeling like pure heaven.

He pulled back, his hand stroking her cheek. "And that's why we're a good idea. Now, can we go hang out and relax? That's all I want. Just to be with you while I can."

She treated him to a forced grin, and he was determined that by the end of the day, her smile would be for real.

They exited the vehicle and grabbed their bags. He'd stopped to pick up sandwiches and drinks, though he knew his mom always kept a stocked fridge. They were only away for two days, so she wouldn't have thrown anything out.

"So this is where I grew up," he said as he let them inside. And though it wasn't always easy to come back here, it was his first home. "And since my place doesn't have a pool, I figured there's no reason not to use it. Come on."

He let them into the house, which was a large home that some people said was in a McMansion type of neighborhood in Connecticut. "My dad's a stockbroker," he said, grasping her hand and leading her through the house. He planned to skip the tour, not wanting to end up in Levi's room. "And Mom was the librarian in the high school. She loved teaching but she's retired now." She left after Levi's death, finding it difficult to be around kids, but again, not something he wanted to bring up to Vivi. "They're awesome people."

"Sounds like you love them a lot. I feel the same way about my mom."

He paused at the linen closet and pulled out some oversized towels before directing her to the sliding doors that led outside. "What about your dad?" he asked, shutting the sliders.

"Here, let me help." She placed her bag down, took the towel, and helped him cover two chairs. "My father was two different people," she said, smoothing nonexistent wrinkles from the towel.

Rising, she faced him. "A great parent to me and a shitty parent to Vic." She held up a hand. "I'm not offering up an excuse. I'm just stating facts because you asked. He died five years ago."

He swallowed hard. "I'm sorry."

"Thank you."

"Vivi … I want to get to know you. If it means hearing about Vic, so be it. I'm never going to get over what happened, but I'm not going to hold it against you."

She glanced up at him. "You're a good man, Landon."

"I'm a man who wants to get to know a woman, period. Now can we enjoy the sun?" He grabbed the bottom of his shirt and pulled it over his head, revealing an already tanned chest and rippled muscles that had her drooling.

She appreciated him lightening the moment. With a grin, she mimicked him, taking off her tee shirt, leaving herself wearing nothing but the skimpy bikini.

"Jesus," he muttered and stepped toward her, hooking an arm around her waist and pulling her to him. "I can't keep my hands off you." He splayed his hands around her waist and settled her between his thighs, his cock pressing directly against her sex.

"What happened to enjoying the pool and the sun?" she asked playfully, writhing against him, letting him know she was as aroused as he was.

"I'm pretty sure we're both enjoying."

She tipped her head back. "We are. But I think we should get back to getting to know each other. She eased out of his grasp and settled onto a towel, stretching that sexy body out on the lounger.

She was killing him but he'd go along for now. "How old were you when you started singing?" he asked.

"Six in a talent show. Then I got the lead in every musical afterwards. The kids hated me. Why did you decide to open a nightclub?"

"Jason's cousin Gabe had connections. He also had the funds to lend us, and everything just fell into place." He straddled the other chair and leaned back, the sun baking on his face. "Tell me about your mom. You're close?"

She nodded. "Mom's a lawyer. She has her own small legal practice, but she likes taking cases for the underprivileged, people who can't afford good representation."

He drew a deep breath and decided to dive in. He couldn't ignore the elephant in the room that was Vic if he wanted a relationship with her. And he did. "Vic said on television that they're estranged, too. Why?" A lot of parents would be in denial or stand by their child no matter what.

Her gaze shot to him in surprise. "Umm, Mom tried really hard when Vic was growing up. She divorced my father because he was such a bully, and she tried to deal with Vic, to discipline him, to rein him in. It never worked. And when he didn't…" She broke off whatever she'd been about to say.

"Go on," he said gruffly.

"When he didn't show any remorse for what happened in college … she couldn't stand by him. Neither of us could."

He nodded in understanding. It said a lot about both Vivi and her mom. "Your father was alive back then."

"Yeah. He refused to pay for a criminal lawyer. Mom said she'd do her best to find someone, and then Vic started defending his actions and Mom walked away. She couldn't live with what he'd done or how he felt about it." She sniffed, the subject clearly upsetting her, and she swiped at her eyes with the backs of her hands.

"Come here."

She rose and stepped to his lounger, straddling it in front of him. "I just don't understand why you think

I'm worth dredging up all these memories. And I'm not someone with low self-esteem. I just come with so much related baggage. Related to you, I mean."

"When my dad met my mom in college, he took one look at her and he knew she was the one for him. When Jason met Faith, same thing. Tanner, the hypocrite? Also the same. So I've seen too many examples for me to walk away from what I feel for you." His heart thudded hard in his chest, emotion he couldn't deny always a part of him when he was around this woman.

"I feel it, too, but I'm leaving, Landon. I can't turn my back on my dream. And your business, family, partners, and friends are all here. I could end up opening for a big name overseas for months on end." She pulled her bottom lip between her teeth, releasing it.

He wanted to lean in and suck on that sensitive flesh, but first he needed her to listen. "I'm not going to worry now about September. I'm not going to deny myself two months with you because I'm worried about the end." He wasn't just risking heartbreak, he was guaranteeing it.

And he still couldn't walk away.

Chapter Seven

AFTER THEIR SERIOUS talk, they grew quiet for a while and Vivi relaxed in the sun, refusing to dwell on anything sad or negative. Landon had brought here to have fun and enjoy his company, and that's what she intended to do. Live in the moment.

And in this moment, she was sticky and sweaty and wanted to cool off. She'd already pulled her hair into a messy bun but she was hot. Rising to her feet, she walked to the pool steps, going in slowly until she realized the water was heated to the perfect temperature to let go and slide in. The water caressed her skin and felt deliciously good as she dipped all the way in up to her shoulders and sighed.

She leaned against the wall and looked out at Landon. His bronzed body glistened beneath the sun, and she wanted to glide her fingers over the spectacular muscles and feel every broad inch of him.

He sat up, shading his eyes with his hand over his sunglasses, studying her in return before rising and walking over, diving into the deep end.

He came up, swam to her, and shook his head, spraying her with water.

"Landon!" she said, laughing, wiping the droplets from her face.

With a sexy grin, he bracketed her against the side of the pool, his arms braced on either side her body. The water came to mid-thigh. "Afraid of a little water?"

She shook her head. "Not at all," she said, sliding her hands to his hips and easing closer to the edge of his waistband. "I like the water and I like being in it with you." Leaning forward, she pressed her lips to his.

He groaned and pulled her against him, the swell of his erection grinding against her sex.

"Mmm. You feel good." She wriggled herself deeper into him.

"You feel amazing. I'm dying to get inside you." He dipped his fingers into the bikini bottoms and began sliding them down her legs.

Wanting the same thing, she helped him, pulling the bottoms off her feet and placing them on the deck of the kidney-shaped pool. When she looked up, he was naked, his thick cock standing at attention in front of her.

She gripped him in her palm and pumped her hand up and down until a drop of pre-come settled on the head.

"Enough," he said in a tight voice.

"What's the matter?" she asked. "You don't like me teasing you?"

"I have no intention of coming in my parents' pool. I much prefer doing it inside of you," he said with a sexy grin. "Now let's move to a chair." He lifted her and she wrapped her arms around his neck as he walked out of the pool, settling her onto the well-cushioned lounger covered by a towel.

She pushed herself back, arching her hips up, her sex gleaming in the sunlight, wet from wanting him.

"Jesus, you're beautiful." He slid a finger through her dampness, ending with a light press on her clit.

She moaned and tipped her head back, clenching herself and feeling empty. "Come on, Landon. I need you."

He stepped closer, grabbed his cock in his hand, and glided it back and forth over her pussy, taking his time, playing and arousing her into an unbearable frenzy.

She narrowed her eyes and mock-glared. "Really? You're going to keep teasing me?"

"Good things are worth the wait," he said in a gruff voice. Nudging himself at her entrance, he placed his hands on her thighs. "Ready?"

"For you?" she asked, looking into his eyes. "Always."

Gripping her skin tightly, with her leaning against the back of the chair, he thrust deep and she saw stars, feeling him everywhere.

"Oh, fuck," he said as he bottomed out inside her.

He slid his hands from her thighs to the sides of the chair and began to glide into her, taking her hard, pleasure filling her so fast she was overwhelmed. He thrust in and out, his hips grinding his pelvis against her every time he entered. Her fingers tangled in his hair, pulling on the silken strands as he took her hard and fast, arousal and emotion fighting for equal footing inside her.

Their connection went soul deep and scared her so much. What was supposed to be a summer fling was going to be hard to keep in that little defined box. Not when they were joined, her body clasping around his and the orgasm of the century beckoning.

He dipped his head, his lips meeting hers, kissing her as he pressed her into the chair cushion, then thrust once, twice, and on the third time, he stilled. His big body shuddered as his orgasm took hold and he came, filling her with his essence. A brief moment of clarity hit her and she realized they hadn't used protection. Knowing she was on the pill helped. Before she could think any more, he reached between them and slid a finger over her sex, pressing hard on her clit, and she shook as her own climax hit.

She toppled over the edge, her entire being swept away by the intense sensations wracking her body. She grasped his shoulders to anchor herself to something in this world, to Landon, the man who was over-whelming her and chipping away at her walls, one piece at a time.

LANDON COLLAPSED ONTO Vivi, out of breath and completely sated but aware he couldn't remain on top of her too long. He pushed himself up and slid out of her, awareness hitting him hard as he stood.

"Shit, Vivi. I didn't use a condom." He didn't let himself panic.

"Yeah. I realized that when it was too late to stop." She looked up at him with trusting eyes. "I'm on the pill."

He blew out a long breath, relieved they didn't have an issue. He hadn't thought about having kids in a long time, and he knew that, for her, now wasn't the right time. Not with her career about to take off. Although he was shocked the fear he'd expect to experience had never kicked in. Vivi pregnant with his kid didn't scare him. Huh. Hell of a thing to think about.

"I'm clean," he said. "I just want you to know you

can trust me. We had physicals for life insurance policies." He and his partners.

"Thank you. Me, too. Yearly physical." She blushed, the discussion obviously not one she felt comfortable having. "Way to kill the moment?"

He shook his head, pulling her up from the chair and into his arms. "Nothing could ever kill the moment with you." He slid his hands to her waist and kissed her lips.

She shot him a grateful smile, then slid out of his embrace and reached for the towel, wrapping it around her waist. "Is there a guest shower?" she asked.

"Of course. Come on. You can use the one I shared with Levi growing up." He was shocked his brother's name slipped so easily off his tongue. Something about being with Vivi eased the jagged edges of pain he'd normally feel even mentioning his twin.

They cleaned up around the pool, her grabbing her suit bottoms off the deck, him taking in the sunscreen and the other towels.

First Vivi showered, then Landon took a quick one, and when he dressed and stepped out of the bathroom, he searched and found Vivi in the laundry room, throwing the towels into the machine. "Give me yours from the shower. I can do everything at once."

He grinned and tossed the damp towels into the

machine. "I planned on running a wash myself."

"It's fine. You can fold it all when we're finished." She winked at him and turned on the washer. "I just didn't want to leave work for your mom."

"Thank you," he murmured.

With the laundry in process, he grasped her hand and led her through the house and into the den, where they could watch TV until they were ready to leave.

He sat down on the couch, his arm around her shoulders, and pulled her close against him. It felt right to have her curled close to him, he thought, breathing in the scent of the strawberry shampoo that they'd used on their hair.

Without warning, the garage door leading to the house opened with a creak and footsteps sounded. "Landon? Are you here? We saw your car parked in the driveway!" his mother called.

"Oh my God." Vivi bolted up from her seat, pulling out of his arms and standing by the sofa. "They're here. Your parents are here," she said, wide-eyed and obviously panicked.

"In the den, Mom!" He rose and grasped Vivi's hand. She stood before him, damp hair falling over her shoulders, wearing her long tee shirt and flip-flops … no underwear, not that his parents would see or know. At least he had on his swimsuit, which was fast-drying. "Calm down."

He reached out and squeezed her hands just as his mother entered the room, his father by her side.

"Landon, what a nice surprise!" his mother, Carrie, said, looking well, her brunette hair growing longer each time he saw her.

"I could say the same. I thought you were going away for the weekend," he said, surprised to see them.

His father, Samuel, waved a hand dismissively and ran a hand through his salt-and-pepper hair. "I'd had enough of being with people," he said of the conference he and his mom had gone to for his work. "We came home early. What are you ... two doing here?" He pointedly looked at Vivi.

Because Landon never brought women to his parents' home.

"We wanted to go for a swim." Grasping Vivi's hand, he squeezed reassuringly. "Mom, Dad, I want you to meet Vivi Zane."

She stepped forward to shake their hand. "It's a pleasure to meet you."

Her parents took her hand in turn.

"The pleasure is ours, young lady," Landon's father said.

Ripping off a Band-Aid was the best way to go, or so his mom had always said. "Vivi is..."

"I work at Landon's club," Vivi quickly chimed in, causing Landon to narrow his gaze.

She glanced at him imploringly, and he read her plea in her expression. *Please don't tell them who I am.* Lying didn't sit well with him, but he completely understood her fear. He might not tell his parents now, but for sure he would when they were alone, giving them time to adjust to the situation before he brought Vivi around them again, knowing she was Vic's sister.

He would have been up-front now, but he respected her shame and embarrassment about Vic's actions. It was his job to convince her that she wasn't her brother and didn't carry his behavior on her shoulders. Of course, given his initial reaction, he was being hypocritical, but he'd come around. And he hoped his parents would as well.

"That's wonderful!" his mother said. "Landon told me about the singer he hired. I can't wait to come by again soon. It's been too long since we had a night out at the club."

Reading the room, or rather Vivi's mood, Landon decided he should take her home. Although he hadn't expected his parents to come home, once they had, he'd hoped they could get to know her. Now clearly wasn't the time.

"We were just about to leave," he said and his mother's expression fell.

"I was hoping that since you were here, you could

stay for dinner." She looked at him hopefully.

Vivi shook her head. "I'm so sorry but I need to be at a rehearsal." She glanced away, not meeting his mother's gaze.

"There will be another time," his dad said. "Right?"

"Right." Landon would make sure of it.

Goodbyes said, with promises that Landon would let them know a good night to come to the club to see Vivi perform, they made their way to the SUV.

The initial ride to the city was silent, Vivi curled close to the door, not speaking. He reached out and put his hand on her thigh. "Hey."

She turned her head and he realized her eyes were red. She'd been trying not to cry.

Unable to help himself, he eased over on the side of the road at the nearest safe spot he could find and cut the engine. He reached over, unbuckled her seat belt, and pulled her close, wrapping his arms around her as much as he could.

To his utter shock, she broke down, full on crying, shaking in his arms. "I hate him," she said into his now wet shirt. "I hate how evil he is. I hate how much he impacts my life even though I didn't do anything wrong."

He smoothed his hand down her back. "Hey, you didn't do anything. That's what you need to remember."

She pushed away from him, blinking back tears. "I can't face your parents. I can't do this. Be with you. It's wrong. You should hate me for being related to him."

"But I don't hate you. And if you hadn't given me a very distinct signal, I would have told my parents who you were." He paused. "I'm not ashamed to be with you."

She swiped her wet eyes with the back of her hand. "Well, maybe you should be." She pushed herself back into her seat. "Your parents don't need a constant reminder."

"Vivi..." He swallowed hard, wondering how to explain this to her without making things worse. "We don't need a reminder because Levi is always with us. We don't forget. We always remember. We just go forward and live our lives the way he'd want us to." He grasped her hand and pulled it into his lap. "And right now, I want to live it with you."

When she didn't respond right away, he knew she needed time to process, so he put the car in drive and headed back to the club. He walked her to her door and kissed her before watching her go inside. As she shut the door behind him, he had the sense she thought she was shutting him out. Too bad she didn't know the lengths to which he'd go to get what he wanted. And he really wanted Vivi to be a part of his life.

Unfortunatley it was impossible to bring someone into his life who didn't want to be there. Or maybe she wanted to be with him but didn't think she deserved the chance because of who she was related to. The end result was the same, which meant he had to figure out a way to step up his game.

TANNER CALLED LANDON to meet him at the gym. The place had been in existence forever, the inside old, but the owner was a good guy and Tanner liked to support him. Plus he'd made friends and had sparring partners here.

Landon arrived to find Jason already there and Tanner pulling on his boxing gloves.

"Hey." He joined the men outside the ring. "Everything okay?" Because they usually met up at the club unless something was on Tanner's mind that he needed to work out on the mat.

Jason shot Landon a glance. "Not for me to tell," he said, his gaze falling on Tanner.

"Scarlett's pregnant." He dropped the news as if it were a bomb going off.

"That's great news!" He glanced at his friend's concerned expression. "Isn't it?"

Tanner examined the laces on his gloves. "If I'm a good father, it is. But what do I know about being a decent parent? My own dad kicked the shit out of me and verbally treated me like dirt."

Landon and Jason exchanged glances. "I think you just answered your own concern," Landon told him, placing a hand on his shoulder for support. He knew Tanner had a shitty upbringing and understood his concern, but Tanner was one of the best men he knew. "You would never do that to your kid."

"Of course not. I'm just ... I'm fucking scared." He dropped his hands and lowered himself to the nearest bench.

Joining him, Landon sat down beside his friend. "You've got this. You know that, right? I mean, if you want to get into the ring and pound something, go ahead, but before you do, I have a question. What did you do when Scarlett told you?"

He swallowed hard. "Said I was excited. Kissed her."

"And ran for the gym?" Jason asked from where he leaned against the ropes.

Tanner ducked his head.

"Okay, you're going home to talk to your fiancée, so gloves off." Reaching over, Landon yanked at the laces, releasing the tight hold. "Scarlett knows you, so I'm sure she's okay, but you two need to deal with this together."

Jason nodded in agreement. "I also suggest you think about setting a wedding date. I know Scarlett is a workaholic and you indulge her but–"

"I already planned to do that," Tanner said. "After I released my panic in here. But you're right. I need to be better for Scarlett." He held a hand out for Landon to pull off his first glove, after which he jerked off the second one. "I'm going home."

Landon grinned, glad his good deed was done for the day. He wanted to get back to the club and catch Vivi after her rehearsal.

"But before we go, is everything okay with you?" Tanner asked as he repacked his gym bag.

He'd been hoping to avoid this conversation, but he might as well lay it out there. "I took Vivi swimming at my folks'. They were supposed to be away for the weekend but they came home early."

"Shit," Jason muttered, rocking back on his heels. "Did you introduce them for real?"

"I wanted to. Hell, I was about to when she jumped in with an explanation about working at our club. She did not want be outed as Vic's sister. And when we got into the car, she broke down. Totally fell apart because of what telling my parents would do to them and remind them of."

It'd killed him to see her like that ... and though

thinking about Levi was always like a knife in his heart, he'd learned to live with the emptiness and pain. How to explain to Vivi that she was starting to help him heal in a way he never had before? He'd never believed he'd be able to live a full life without his twin, but she'd given him back music, warmth, and love.

Love? He mentally reared back. He couldn't possibly be there just yet with her … could he?

Tanner pulled out a sport drink bottle from his bag and took a long sip. "Shit. I really misjudged her. I'm sorry, man."

Landon tipped his head. "I know it's hard to wrap your head around my feelings for her." He was struggling with understanding how he could fall so hard so fast himself. "But she's empathetic and understanding. And this whole situation is eating away at her. She doesn't want to get involved with me because of it," he muttered, frustrated.

"So what's your plan?" Jason asked. "Because you always have a plan."

With a grin, Landon glanced at his friends. "I'm going to pull her into my life despite her fears. First up, I plan to talk to my parents, give them time to come to terms, and then let them get to know her. If she's leaving at the end of the summer, I want all the time I can get with her before she goes."

He saw the way his friends looked at each other.

Heard the words they didn't say because he was thinking them himself. Why was he investing so much time and effort into an affair that had a built-in end date?

Because he didn't *want* it to end.

Long-distance relationships could work, couldn't they?

After leaving, the guys went their separate ways and Landon headed to the club. As he thought, he'd missed rehearsal, having been busy this morning meeting with a supplier, then the trip to the gym, so he headed up the elevator and knocked on Vivi's door.

He thought he heard sounds inside but after the knock, silence. Frowning, he banged harder, wondering if she'd really ignore him or if she'd gone out.

"Vivi!" He knocked harder.

When she didn't answer, he decided to give her the benefit of the doubt that she wasn't home. Not that he really believed it.

But he wasn't giving up.

✧   ✧   ✧

"YOU'RE AN IDIOT." Ellie popped a piece of popcorn into her mouth and followed it up with a sip of water. "That man obviously cares about you and you ignored him. Explain."

Narrowing her gaze, Vivi put the television back

on because she'd shut it off when Landon began knocking. "I already explained this to you. The sight of me can only cause him and the people around him pain."

"Obviously he doesn't think so."

"Well, he hasn't told his parents yet. And I'm guessing his partners are tolerating me for his sake. Look, I'm not trying to be stubborn. I am a living, breathing, walking reminder of Victor and, as a result, of Levi Bennett's death."

Ellie curled her legs beneath her on the sofa and frowned. "I don't deny that his parents may not be overly accepting at first—"

"Or at all." She twisted her fingers together until they hurt. The very thought of facing his parents' grief-stricken faces... "Even after all this time, one look at me will bring their pain rushing back."

Ellie's expression softened. "You may be right. I just feel like you're giving up too easily."

"You want me to forget what my brother did?" she asked, horrified.

She shook her head. "I want you to remember you didn't have any part of it. And admit you deserve to be happy. Wherever you find that happiness."

Happiness. Deserving it was one thing, but finding it with the man whose heart was so big he was willing to see her and not her brother? How was that fair to anyone?

"Do you want to miss out on this chance with Landon?" Ellie eyed her with that all-knowing gaze.

"Of course that's not what I want." Settling into the opposite side of the sofa, Vivi curled into the corner and wondered if her friend had a point.

She wasn't responsible for her brother's crimes. She knew that. She just didn't want to bring up bad memories for Landon and his family. But for the summer, should she reach for the man she desired? Give herself some wonderful memories of her own before she left for wherever she and Owen decided was best for her career?

"Well?" Ellie tossed a piece of popcorn at her.

Vivi picked up the popped kernel and slipped it into her her mouth. "I'll think about it," she promised, meaning it. Because she didn't think she could stay away from him no matter how much she thought it was best for him.

LANDON HAD A plan. But as he approached his parents' house, his certainty that they'd ultimately come to accept and understand he had feelings for Victor Clark's sister wavered. Shoring up his nerves, he parked his SUV and headed up the shrub-lined path leading to the front door, where his mom greeted him.

"Landon! I was so surprised when you asked if you could talk to us. You don't need a reason to come home." His mother embraced him and he hugged her back, inhaling the familiar scent that he associated with his childhood.

His mom was a creature of habit, and he supposed it was a good thing that the company still manufactured her favorite perfume. It also made her birthday and Christmas easier on him.

He stepped back, taking in his mom in her dark jeans and pink blouse, matching shoes on her feet. She looked younger than her years and ... happy. Was he going to burst the bubble of sanity she'd finally managed to find? Was Vivi right about keeping them in the dark?

"Landon? Obviously something is bothering you?" his mother said, shutting the door behind him. "Come on. Let's go into the kitchen. That's always been our place." Smiling at him, she turned and led the way into the sunny room with an eat-in breakfast nook.

He pulled out a chair and sat down, not surprised when his mom walked over with a plate of home-baked chocolate chip cookies and put them down in front of him. "Your favorite."

"Levi's, too," he said, remembering how his brother would steal a few and take them into his room despite the no-eating-in-the-bedroom rule.

He picked one up and bit into it, unable to stop the moan that came from his throat. "God, they're still warm."

"You said you were coming for a visit. I baked."

"I love you, Mom." A lump formed in his throat, more because of his twin's absence than the statement he'd just made. God, this was going to be so much harder than he'd thought.

Carrie settled into a chair beside him. "Is this about the woman you brought here?"

He looked up, surprised although he shouldn't be. His mother always had a sixth sense when it came to her ... boys. "Yeah, it is about Vivi."

"Pretty name," his mother said. "Beautiful woman."

"Yes." He ran a hand over the top of his head. "Umm, I think Dad should be here for this."

She raised her eyebrows in surprise. "You're not getting married, are you?" Her hand came to rest on her heart, maybe in hope, maybe in panic.

He couldn't be sure, but he burst out laughing. "No, nothing like that." But his gut said telling them about impending matrimony would be simpler than this.

"Samuel!" she called. "Landon's here and wants to talk! He'd just gotten out of the shower when you arrived."

160

A few minutes later, footsteps sounded from the stairs and his father joined them. After the father-son greeting and his mother instructing her husband to take a seat, they both looked at Landon and waited.

Unable to sit still, he rose to his feet and began pacing. "So Mom already figured out this is about Vivi. The woman you met the other day," he clarified.

His father shot him an amused grin. "Figured that out already, son. What is it? Did you knock her up?"

"Samuel!" his mother said before the words obviously sank in and she turned to Landon. "Did you?" she asked hopefully.

The woman did want grandchildren. That much he knew.

"No, I did not get her pregnant. Jesus." Although the thought didn't bother him as much as it should, which reminded him why he was here, putting them all through this. He cleared his throat and faced them. "You met Vivi the other day."

"Yes. And from the few minutes we spent with her, she's lovely," his mother said.

"Right. The thing is…" He shoved his hands into his front pants pocket. "You met her as Vivi Zane. That's her mother's maiden name. Her birth name is Vivienne Clark."

He dropped the name and waited to see if they put two and two together on their own.

His mother narrowed her gaze and looked to Samuel, but neither said a word. Unable to wait, he blurted out the rest. "Clark, as in Victor Clark. She's his sister."

Shock registered in his parents' faces. Obviously they'd been struggling to make the connection before. After all, it wasn't like they went around thinking Victor's name all the time. If anything, they tried to forget. And Landon hadn't told them about the situation with Victor and their club, protecting them … the way Vivi had wanted to do now.

God, what had he been thinking? "You know what? Never mind. She's leaving at the end of the summer and you won't have to be in the same room with her again," he rushed to say.

"Landon, sit down," his father said in his stern, parental voice.

"Yeah. Okay." He lowered himself back into his seat and decided to lay it all out for them, sparing them asking questions. "When Vivi and I first met, neither one of us knew who the other was. She made the connection first and tried not to take the job we'd offered, but I pushed because she was that talented and good for the club."

He tapped his foot against the floor while his parents listened in silence. "And probably because I was really attracted to her. When I found out, I lost my

162

shit. Trashed my apartment. Tanner and Jason had to come calm me down." His mouth ran dry, and he picked up the glass of water his mother had put down at some point and took a long sip.

"Why didn't she tell you once she knew?" his father asked in a gruff voice.

"It's complicated. I'd insinuated her taking the job could help us out of a bind we'd been in... She thought she could sing, bring in customers, and then leave after the summer ended with no one figuring it out." He swallowed hard, his hands entwined on the table. "Look, I was going to bite the bullet and tell you the truth the day you met her, but she panicked and I could see she wasn't ready. She doesn't want to dredge up pain and bad memories for you."

"Smart girl," his father said bitterly.

Landon didn't blame him. "But she's not her brother. In fact, neither she nor her mother has a relationship with Victor at all. Vivi is different. She's special. And I can't seem to stay away from her." His heart thudded painfully in his chest as he faced the two people who, along with his friends, had been his lifeline when his twin was suddenly gone, brutally taken from him. From all of them.

"God, Landon. Of all the women in the world, you fall for the one whose brother was responsible for Levi's death?" his father asked. *How could you* went without saying.

"The heart wants what the heart wants." His mother, who'd been silent until now, spoke up, her words taking Landon off guard.

"Seriously, Carrie? You're okay with this?" Samuel rose to his feet, shoving the chair roughly under the table, the noise causing a rough squeak.

"I didn't say that."

His mother's sad eyes were filled with tears, and guilt swarmed inside him for bringing this to them at all. "Maybe Vivi was right and we can't work."

Landon's heart squeezed in his chest at the thought of losing Vivi, but choosing between her and his family? That wasn't a notion he'd considered. Damn, but he'd been naïve in thinking he could explain and his parents would just understand.

He and Vivi had other obstacles, and he would deal with the end of the summer when it came, but making the choice to let her go? He couldn't do it.

Reaching out, his mother put her hand over his. "Landon, you think this girl is that special?"

He closed his eyes and pictured Vivi's beautiful face, freckled nose, and wide, hot-chocolate-colored eyes. The hauntingly beautiful sound of her voice. What she'd given him back in life. More than that, he thought about her big heart and the fact that she was trying to do right by his parents in staying away.

"Yeah, I do."

With a growl, his father started to walk out.

"Samuel, stop." Carrie's order echoed in the room.

Pausing, he looked back at his wife.

"We have one son left," Carrie said, meeting Landon's gaze. "And his heart is obviously invested in this woman. I'm not saying I'm happy about the situation, but I'm not going to make him choose."

Landon shot a grateful look at his mom. His strong mother, who always held his family together through the most awful of crises.

"I need time to digest this," Samuel muttered.

"I understand." Landon expected his father to storm from the room, but taking him by surprise, Samuel pulled Landon into a fatherly hug.

"You aren't making it easy, son." Samuel slapped him on the back.

"I know, Dad. Believe me, I know." But with everything in him, he believed Vivi was worth it.

Chapter Eight

VIVI LOVED THE stage. She loved singing to an audience and the live feedback she received when she performed. It didn't matter if she closed her eyes or looked out over the people clapping and singing along, the music floated through her, the words coming out with power and feeling.

As the weeks at Club TEN29 passed, more and more paparazzi and reporters began following her when she left the club, snapping pictures of her wherever she went. Her Instagram followers soared, and Owen urged her to be more open about herself online.

Life was changing at a crazy fast pace.

When she was younger, her mother took her to festivals and she used YouTube to perform for people online, slowly growing an audience. At sixteen, she would find bars willing to let her sing, but she wasn't lucky enough to be discovered then. Her mom needed to work, and though she'd wanted to audition for the singing competition television shows, she'd had no one to take her. By age eighteen, she'd decided to work at coffee shops during the day and perform at night where she could, just enjoying having music in her life. And then her viral moment of fame happened. The nights at Club TEN29 were like a dream, and she didn't take any one of them for granted.

Two weeks had passed since Landon banged on her door looking for her, and he hadn't returned since. The nights she played at the club, he sat at the bar or walked the floor, always watching her, his eyes devouring every inch of her body, but he kept a physical distance that had become painful. And though she was the one who'd insisted they didn't belong together, this separation wasn't working for her. Not if she had to see him all weekend and long for him during the week.

So she came to a decision. For the duration of the summer, she wanted to be with him. She needed his hands on her bare skin and his lips hard on hers. She wanted time to talk to him, to curl up in his arms, and to take advantage of the very limited time they had left. But it was her turn to convince him that she'd changed her mind.

After her last performance of the weekend, she headed upstairs, showered, and cleaned up before sliding into a club-appropriate short dress and high heels and taking the elevator back downstairs with every intention of seducing her man.

✧　✧　✧

EVERY NIGHT VIVI took the stage, her performance was more stellar than the evening before. Landon watched Owen eyeing his prize possession, as he no doubt viewed her, and taking meetings while she sang. Axel Matsen, the douchebag, had become a weekly fixture at the club, no doubt reminding Owen he was in the bidding for whatever choice he brought to Vivi for her future when her time at Club TEN29 came to an end.

And because his parents were still reluctant to embrace his decision, at least his father was, Landon stayed away. Although he was an adult and capable of making his own decisions for his life, this situation was delicate and needed to be handled with care. Losing a child wasn't the same as parents who just disapproved of his choices, and he was trying to be respectful of that. Hell, nobody missed his twin on a soul-deep level more than Landon. Levi had been and still was a part of him.

However, he'd made his decision and time was running out. Tomorrow he would be letting his parents know he loved them, he respected them, but he was going after the woman he cared about because there was every chance he only had precious summer weeks left to be with her.

Jason and Tanner hadn't come in tonight. They were home with their women, something that was becoming more common and not a problem because they had solid management in place. Landon was here tonight for one reason only. For Vivi.

Except after her performance, she'd gone up to her apartment for the night, leaving him down here to brood about how he was going to make his move. Suddenly the elevator door opened and Vivi stepped out, taking his breath away.

She wore a short red dress and killer spiked heels, her hair fell around her shoulders, and she looked around as if she was on a mission. As soon as her gaze landed on his, her purpose became clear.

She strode over to him, hips swaying, sidestepping people, and ignoring the attentive stares of men who couldn't take their gazes off the seductress in red who only had eyes for him. His cock stood up and took notice.

She came up to him and seated herself not next to him but on his lap, where she couldn't help but feel the hard ridge of his erection.

To keep her there without falling, he settled a hand on her hip. "Vivi—"

She cut him off with a finger over his lips. "Shh. I want to go first."

He nipped her finger with his teeth and she

moaned.

"You're not going to distract me, Landon. I've done a lot of thinking about us and I miss you." She ran a finger down his cheek to the collar of his shirt and dipped it inside. "It's been hard singing on that stage, knowing you're out there watching but I can't have you."

His heart slammed hard against his chest. He'd assumed he'd have a difficult time convincing her to be with him again, yet here she was, telling him she wanted him, too.

"You do realize it was your decision to end whatever we'd started," he reminded her.

Her pretty lips pursed into a pout. "I made the wrong choice. You see, I've been thinking. I still think a relationship between us could hurt your family, but since I'm only here for the summer, I thought we could be together, quietly. Just the two of us until I have to leave."

Under any other circumstances, he'd be insulted, but he understood the reason behind the request. And since he was still working on getting his parents to accept her in his life, it was to his benefit to agree to her request. She didn't have to know he planned to continue to seduce her so thoroughly, if she thought she missed him now, she'd go crazy when they were apart. He'd do his damndest to get her to agree to maintain their relationship when the residency ended.

His free hand came to rest on her other hip. "Okay, Vivi, we'll do it your way."

She looked at him in surprise. Clearly she'd thought she'd have more of an uphill battle in order to get him to agree. He'd give her this because he planned to win the war. The one for her heart and her soul.

FOR THE FIRST time in weeks, Vivi felt like she could breathe. With her arms around Landon, his heart beating against her chest, and his hard erection pressing into her thigh, life righted itself again.

"Come dance with me," he said into her ear, his warm breath dancing over the delicate shell, causing her to shiver.

She'd expected him to take her upstairs to bed, not stake his claim on the dance floor. "That's not being discreet," she murmured.

He let out a low chuckle. "My family isn't here. Neither are my partners, though they understand about us now. Come on." He slid her off his lap and rose to his feet, taking her hand and pulling her into the crowded space.

He settled his arms securely around her waist, and despite the steady thumping beat of the music, he held her to him and swayed back and forth as if a slow, crooning song was playing around them. They weren't the only ones wrapped up in each other, but she only had eyes for Landon, and soon she was lost in the warmth of his blue-eyed gaze and the inner strength of the man holding her.

"Sexy dress," he said, his fingers skimming over her bare back. "Did you choose it just for me?"

She couldn't stop her smile. "What do you think?"

"That you rode that elevator and strode through the club like a heat-seeking missile." His hand slid up her back until he cupped her neck, his touch sure and steadying.

"What can I say? Once I decide I want something, very little will stop me. And Landon?" she asked, her own hands slipping inside his jacket and grasping on to the back waistband of his slacks. "I want you."

His low groan reverberated through her. "I'll tell you what. I'll give you what you want if you agree to go out with me tomorrow. You don't need to work at night, and your performances are so good you can take a day without rehearsal."

She narrowed her gaze. "You're trying to seduce me into dating you. *After* we agreed to keep us on the down low."

His boyish grin charmed her. "So?" he asked.

"So we agreed to keep things quiet–"

He silenced her with his mouth, his lips coming down on hers. Yep. Seducing her, she thought, his talented tongue gliding back and forth against hers. Without a struggle, she caved, kissing him back, giving them both what they wanted.

Desire rushed through her, their mouths melding, the feeling of perfection settling in her chest.

"Do we have an agreement?" He separated them just enough to ask.

She slicked her tongue over her damp bottom lip, taking pleasure in how his gaze followed the movement. "Yes. We do." She couldn't resist him, didn't want to. If that meant going out on a date, she'd do it. Summer would come to an end soon enough. Might as well gather up all the time with Landon she could get.

"And that was easier than I thought," he said, pleased. Taking her by surprise, he bent, picked her up, and hefted her over his shoulder until she hung upside down.

"Landon! I'm flashing the room!" she cried out, both shocked and mortified.

His hand came down hard on her ass ... and stayed there, holding her dress in place, which was a good thing since she wore barely there bikini briefs that didn't cover her cheeks.

"Caveman much?" she asked as he strode through the club to cheers and wolf whistles.

"I've been waiting weeks for you to come to your senses. I wasn't about to fight the urge when it struck." He stepped into the elevator and, once they were alone, put her down, holding her until she caught her balance.

Dizziness swept over her, and though she knew a fair portion had to with her quick switch of positions, another chunk was solely due to the passionate expression etched into his handsome features. "Landon." She stroked his cheek with her hand.

The elevator came to a halt and the door opened. Landon grabbed her hand and pulled her toward her apartment, waited as she let them inside, and slammed the door behind them.

Next thing she knew, he'd lifted her over his shoulder once more, this time for the short walk to the bedroom, walking to the other room with determined strides. "You know this can't become a habit?" she asked with a laugh.

"Why not?"

She squeezed his ass, which was mighty fine even from her upside-down position, and held her breath as he flipped her back over and tossed her onto the bed.

She bounced on the mattress and got her bearings, grinning up at him as he stripped out of his clothing. She watched as he bared himself, his tanned, muscled chest, well-defined arms that she couldn't wait to have wrapped around her, and then the impressive rest of his sculpted body. His erection indicated how much he desired her. As much as she wanted him.

Rising onto her knees, she turned and looked over her shoulder, meeting his gaze. "Unzip me, please."

His eyes darkened as he stepped closer and reached for her zipper. But first he gathered her long hair into his hand and swept it to one side, tugging on the strands, a pull she felt deep in her core, her bikini underwear damp with desire.

She kicked off her shoes and they fell to the floor, then shimmied out of the dress, letting the garment drop to her waist. He helped her slide it down her legs, hooking his fingers in her panties and taking them off along with the dress. Before she could process the fact that she was nearly naked, he reached up and unhooked her bra, tossing it aside.

"Turn around," he said in a gruff voice.

Her body responded, her nipples puckering into tight buds. Swallowing hard, she slowly spun to face him, her knees still bent on the mattress. Placing his hands on her shoulders, he dipped his head and placed his mouth on her breast, his lips around her nipple, and began to suck.

The sensations struck hard and fast, and she swayed on the bed, only his strong hands on her waist holding her in place. While his mouth aroused her, incredible sensations fluttering in her belly and throbbing between her thighs, he began to roll and play with her other nipple with his fingertips. She gasped and braced her hands on his shoulders, letting him work her into an unbearable frenzy of heat and need.

"You taste so good," he said, lowering his hand from her breast to cup her sex. "And you feel so hot and wet for me."

He kissed his way down her body, and eventually she succumbed, collapsing onto the bed. She maneuvered so she was lying flat, legs spread, and his face came down between her thighs. Next thing she knew, he was devouring her, licking, tasting, acting as if she was the best treat he'd ever had.

He slid a finger inside her and pumped it in and out until her hips writhed on the bed and her head was moving from side to side. "Landon, please, more. Harder."

He complied, and soon she was dying from the amazing sensations traveling through her body, bringing her up, taking her higher. His tongue lapped back and forth over her clit, gentle at first, then harder, nipping lightly and then returning to gentleness once more.

"Come on, Vivi," he said, his finger still inside her. "Come for me."

He clearly had a plan, and making her come was

priority one. No man had ever devoted so much time to making her feel good, and she knew she'd never find a man as devoted to her pleasure as Landon. Which meant she had to enjoy it while she could.

But he was determined and focused, and soon he'd found just the right pressure and rhythm, and the waves crested and consumed her, taking her over the cliff. She came hard, crying out, holding on to his hair and grinding herself against his mouth until she was wrung out.

But he wasn't finished, and one look at the hunger in his expression and she grew ready for him again. He grasped her legs and pulled her toward the edge of the bed, poised himself at her entrance, and thrust inside.

Her nails scored his back as she wrapped her legs around his waist, holding on as he pounded into her. And despite the rough way he took her, she knew, *felt*, there was more going on between them.

"Look at me."

His rough voice penetrated her thoughts, fought through the desire overtaking her body, and she opened her eyes and looked into his oh-so-blue ones. "Hey, handsome."

A sexy grin lifted his lips. "I want you to feel me inside you."

"I do."

"No, I mean feel *me*. Know this is me making love

178

to you."

His words rocked her to her core, making her more aware of him inside her, around her, part of her. This is what she'd been fighting. Because no matter how they felt about each other, too much remained that would keep them apart.

His past.

Her future.

But they had now.

"I do feel you. And I won't forget."

He narrowed his gaze but said nothing, instead began to move inside her, more slowly this time. Really making love to her, engaging her body, heart, and soul.

She didn't understand how she could feel so much for a man she'd known for such a short time. How he could have gotten past her walls and into her heart so quickly. Nor did she comprehend how it could be *this* man. Life just wasn't fair ... to dangle him in front of her knowing she couldn't keep him.

And when he started rocking inside her, she stopped thinking at all. Emotion and desire consumed her as they toppled into a massive climax together.

THE SUMMER PASSED too quickly, days turning into steamy, sexy nights, Landon always by Vivi's side. For a woman who was used to being alone, she'd quickly grown accustomed to having him around, along with the paparazzi who tried to be her new best friend. But as for Landon, she'd miss him when she was on tour, which, according to Owen, was imminent after she finished up at Club TEN29.

They had a meeting scheduled next week to sit down and discuss actual offers he had in hand. Excitement fluttered through her veins with the knowledge her dream was about to become reality. Ellie promised to go with her wherever the future led, which made Vivi happy. She'd have her assistant/best friend nearby and she wouldn't be by herself in strange cities around the country.

She swallowed hard and focused on tonight's show. She had a feeling Axel would be in the audience. According to Owen, the promoter's connections would be her key to the big time, which was fine with her as long as the man kept his hands to himself. This business was full of dirtbags who could open doors. She just wasn't about to play that kind of game to get where she dreamed of going.

"Knock knock," Landon said before walking into her dressing room.

"Hi!" She rose to her feet and wrapped her arms around him, pressing her lips to his. He tasted like cinnamon and smelled like the warmest musk.

"Hi yourself. Just wanted to give you a kiss good

luck before you go on."

She grinned. It was a habit they'd gotten into every night. No matter what he was doing or how busy with his partners, he made time to come over and kiss her before she performed. He'd become her good luck charm. Ever since they'd gotten together, her singing sounded better, at least to her ears. Or maybe she was just high on love.

Because she did love Landon. How could she not have fallen for him hard and fast when he'd supported her from the beginning? Once he'd come to terms with who she was related to, he hadn't turned his back on her; instead he'd stepped up his pursuit. The man was sex in a suit, decency and goodness in one hot package. And she'd miss him like crazy when she was gone.

"You ready for tonight?" he asked.

She nodded. Turning away, she looked at the mirror, pulling out a tube of lipstick and reapplying the color. "I'm good to go."

Her cell phone rang from its place on her vanity table, and *MOM* flashed on the screen. Knowing her mother wouldn't call this close to show time unless it was important, she answered, hitting the accept button.

"Hi, Mom, you're on speakerphone. What's up?" She smiled at Landon as she spoke.

"Hey, baby girl. It's about Vic. Your brother." Her mother's voice broke on the word. "He was killed in prison."

"What? Dead? Victor's dead?" she asked, dazed by the news.

His face a mask, Landon grabbed a chair and gently lowered her into it, keeping a hand on her shoulder.

Her mother sniffled over the phone. "Apparently the other inmates don't take it well when someone snitches on a cellmate to get themselves out early." As her brother had done prior to his current parole violation and return to jail.

Oh, God. "Mom, I'll be right over. You shouldn't be alone."

"Yeah, that would be good, honey. Thank you."

It wasn't like her mother to admit to needing her, so Vivi knew she had to be there. "I'll see you soon." She disconnected the call and looked up at Landon, knowing better than to expect sympathy from him when it came to losing her brother but wanting his arms around her anyway.

No doubt he was happy Victor was dead.

As for Vivi? How should she feel right now? Vic had been her sibling, albeit estranged. A boy who'd tormented her, a man who'd used her. But they were related by blood, and her mother, for certain, was grieving her son.

182

"I have to go. I'm sorry about the performance but my mother needs me," she said in a choked voice. Tears formed in her eyes and took her by surprise.

Landon managed a nod. "Of course. Go," he said in a neutral tone that squeezed her heart.

Doing her best not to show him that he'd hurt her, she gathered her purse and her cell and pulled up the Uber app.

Landon didn't stop her when she walked out to meet the car.

VIVI HELD IT together until she reached her mother's house and fell into her waiting arms. Together they cried for the little boy Vic had been before their father's belittling and fists had changed him.

"It's my fault, you know." Her mother placed a hand on the baby book she'd been turning the pages on, brushing her fingers across her son's footprints and all his firsts.

"What's your fault? Staying with Dad? Because I know you were scared to leave," Vivi murmured.

For all Anne Marie's professional strength, it hadn't extended to her personal life, where she'd let Victor Senior walk all over her. And abuse his son. Vivi had read enough self-help books about abuse not to blame her mother, but she was sure her brother hadn't felt the same way.

Her mother swallowed hard. "I will never excuse your brother's behavior, but I do blame myself for not getting him out of that situation when he was a child." She drew a deep breath, her eyes damp with tears. "Your father treated Vic the way he did because he wasn't his real son, something he didn't find out until after we'd named him Victor Junior."

"What?" Vivi sat back in her seat. "Did you just say—"

Nodding, her mother said, "I had an affair. I don't know if you remember, but life wasn't always hard with your father. It started after Vic was born ... after he found a letter in my dresser from the man I'd been seeing. He put the pieces together. He blamed me and he couldn't look at your brother without seeing a reminder."

Brushing at the tears on her face with the back of her hand, Vivi looked at her mother, seeing her with new eyes. "Why didn't you leave him then?"

"Guilt over the affair. The fact that I'd made wedding vows and meant them at the time. And your father always promised he'd get over my betrayal."

He never did. And he'd always taken it out on Vic. God, what a mess, Vivi thought. But she wasn't going to blame her mother or lose the only family she had left.

"We need to make decisions about Vic now," her mother said and Vivi knew what she meant.

"I think we should have a quiet burial. Just you and me. Lay him to rest." And go on. It wasn't like she'd had a relationship with her sibling, but like her mother, she felt the loss.

Not that Landon had seemed to understand or even care. His light touch on her shoulder hadn't exactly been compassionate. Although a part of her couldn't blame him, there was still the fact that they were in an intense relationship that she thought went beyond physical attraction.

This was exactly the kind of situation she'd feared. The notion of his parents finding out who she was and hating her for being Vic's sister, and now she was grieving and the man she loved couldn't find it in his heart to be there for her. And she couldn't even be angry at him for it.

"I think a family-only burial is a good idea," her mother said, breaking into her thoughts. "I'll make the arrangements," she said, choking over the word.

With a nod, Vivi tried not to think about how difficult it was going to be to put her brother in the ground without Landon by her side. She was going to be there to shore up her mother and help her get through the loss of her son.

But who would be there for Vivi?

185

✧   ✧   ✧

LANDON JOINED TANNER and Jason at the bar, his heart with Vivi as she walked herself out the door and to the Uber that waited to take her to her mother's place. He couldn't go with her and pretend to care that she mourned the bastard who'd killed his twin. But he should have been there for her, to help her through her pain.

How?

How the fuck did he do it?

"Landon? What's wrong? You're pale as fuck and you look like you've seen a ghost."

He swallowed over the lump in his throat. "Pour me a shot."

Tanner narrowed his gaze. "Since when do you drink?"

"Vic's dead. Now pour me a shot of whiskey."

Eyes narrowed, Tanner poured and slid the glass across the bar.

"What do you mean Vic's dead?" Jason asked, leaning in on the counter.

Around them, the crowd danced and thought they were going to see their big act tonight. One of them would have to go onstage and disappoint the people, but a death in the family was an understandable reason for a cancellation.

Landon blew out a breath and repeated what Vivi's mother had told her without feeling the sense of satisfaction he once thought he'd experience if the bastard turned up dead. Instead he was worried about Vivi, but instead of being there for her, he'd frozen inside.

"Hell, we should all do a shot," Tanner said, pouring two more and raising his glass. "To Levi."

Landon raised his gaze. "My brother wouldn't celebrate Vic's death, and fuck, but I can't either." Nausea filled him at the all the emotions whirling inside him, each fighting for dominance.

"Where's Vivi?" Jason asked, and Landon shot him a grateful glance for thinking of his girl.

He curled his fingers into tight fists. "I fucked up. She got the call from her mother and took an Uber to be with her. I was paralyzed with shock and relief, mostly, which makes me feel guilty now. I'm glad her brother is dead. By the time my head and heart kicked back online and I accepted that this was a loss for her, she was gone."

"Okay, I say we do the shots anyway. This is an occasion to mark, one way or another. We no longer have to worry about the bastard in this world," Tanner said.

Needing something to ease his pain, Landon lifted the glass and downed it in one gulp, feeling the unfamiliar burn in his chest. It'd been a long while since he'd drunk. He and the guys knew how ironic it was that they didn't consume alcohol yet owned a bar. But the opportunity had arisen and it worked for them.

With a glance at one another, Jason and Tanner also finished their shot.

Tanner nodded in satisfaction. "Now what are you going to do about Vivi?" he asked.

Knowing he'd made a royal mess of things, Landon hung his head. "I should have done something more than put a hand on her shoulder like a stranger would. I should have told her I'm sorry. Except I'm not. I am sorry for her loss but not that Vic is dead, and that really complicates things." He blew out a breath, surprised life could take such a drastic turn in a matter of minutes. Then again, hadn't he learned that lesson years ago?

Jason frowned at him. "I think you need to get your head on straight and figure out how you're going to handle everything when it comes to Vivi. From the end of this gig to the death of her brother. Either you're in and you're there for her ... or you're not, and everyone, even Vivi, would understand why."

"You're not suggesting I go to a funeral for the bastard?" Landon asked, horrified.

"No. I don't think even Vivi would expect that."

188

Except he hadn't seen the look on her face when he'd just told her to go. No emotion, no expression, nothing. True, she'd tried to hide the hurt, but he'd seen the pain flowing through her anyway.

Fuck.

"I need to let my parents know about Vic," he said, addressing the other thing on his mind because figuring out how to deal with this situation with Vivi wasn't something he knew how to do.

At least not right now.

Chapter Nine

ON A RAINY day in a New Jersey cemetery, Vivi and her mother buried Vic beside her father. Rain dripped down her face, and sadness consumed her for the life he'd lived and the one he'd lost and for all the pain and havoc he'd caused during his time on earth. She ignored the *snap snap* of the cameras and the flashes taking gratuitous shots even here, at a burial.

She'd taken time off from the club and had Owen tell Landon and his partners she'd be back next weekend, which happened to be her second-to-last one at Club TEN29. Needing time to herself, she'd packed a bag and gone to stay at her mother's for a little while.

At her mom's, she'd woken up after a night spent tossing and turning and joined her mother in the kitchen. Sunlight shone through the window over the sink and sliding glass doors behind the table. Her mother lived in a small house in Queens, an easy enough trip to Manhattan and the law office where her mom worked.

Anne Marie handed her a coffee mug with cream and sugar, and Vivi gratefully took a long sip. "Mmm. I needed that."

"I hear you. Can I get you something to eat?" Tucking a strand of her dark hair behind her ear, her mom waited for her to answer.

Vivi shook her head. "I'll pour myself some cereal."

She'd also taken this week to eat and do whatever she wanted, no exercise, no practice, no dieting to fit into her stage outfits. She walked to the pantry and pulled out a box of Honey Nut Cheerios and grabbed the almond milk from the fridge. Okay, maybe she'd be a little healthy.

"Have you heard from him?" her mother asked.

Vivi brought everything to the table and settled into the seat across from her mom. "Have I heard from who?" she asked, playing dumb. She didn't really think she'd be putting her mother off, but she sure could give not talking about Landon her best shot.

Her mother's disappointed frown had Vivi squirming in her seat like a badly behaving teenager.

"Fine. No, I haven't heard from him."

Ever since she'd gotten the call about Vic's death, Landon had disappeared. She hadn't gotten in touch with him, either, but regardless of the situation, she was the one grieving. He could reach out to check on her if he cared enough. In the wake of his silence, she drew her own conclusions and they weren't good ones.

She poured the cereal into the bowl, followed by the milk, picked up a spoon, and dug in.

"Maybe he doesn't know what to say." Ever the devil's advocate, her mother offered up an excuse.

Vivi wasn't buying it, and she felt the weight of her mother's stare until Vivi met her gaze. "Even if that's true, he hurt me," she admitted.

There'd been a reason she wasn't sleeping well, and Landon's sudden absence from her life explained it.

"This is between Landon and me, not Landon and Vic." And if they were going to have a relationship of any kind, her feelings, no matter what they stemmed from, had to matter. "It's over anyway. I'm meeting with Owen this week to discuss my future, and it can't be in New York."

"Whoa." Anne Marie held up a hand. "Let's break this down, shall we?" her mother the lawyer said, in her educational tone, causing Vivi to frown. "Let's start with you and Landon. What do you want from him, Vivienne? Your brother killed his twin. I think you need to meet him halfway."

She shook her head. "I need to know he can handle who I am, Mom. Especially now that Vic is gone. There is no longer a chance that he can get out of jail or torment Landon and his friends, or try to insinuate himself in my life somehow. In a strange way, I'm free and clear. If Landon wanted me, he'd find a way to show me that."

Her mother took a long sip of her coffee. "I can't argue with your logic," she said at last.

"Which makes the fact that I'll be leaving town irrelevant. Things are already over." Her stomach twisted at the thought of never being in Landon's arms again. Still, they'd been a shaky couple from the start, and she'd warned him of that very fact. He just hadn't wanted to listen.

"I just want you to be happy." Her mother held out her arms. "Come give me a hug."

With a small smile, Vivi rose and wrapped her arms around her mother, who needed the emotional embrace as much as Vivi did, and then they each pulled back. Vivi sat back down with her cereal and dove in.

The doorbell rang and her mom looked surprised. "I wonder who that could be." Rising, she went to answer it, and Vivi heard low voices from the other room.

Vivi took another spoonful just as her mother returned to the kitchen with a guest in tow.

Landon met her gaze, a look of remorse on his handsome face. He wore a pair of dark jeans and a navy tee shirt, his muscles bulging from the edges of the short sleeves. No matter how often she laid eyes on him, he impacted her as if it were the first time. His well-groomed good looks took her breath away.

"Well, look who I found on the doorstep?" Anne Marie put a hand on Landon's bicep and led him farther into the room.

"Vivi," he said in a gruff voice.

"Hi." She narrowed her eyes. "How did you find me?"

A wry smile lifted his lips. "Ellie's an easy bribe with Cronuts." The croissant dough-like pastry that looked like a donut and was filled with various flavors that melted in your mouth was enough to make anyone with a sweet tooth cave.

Vivi wagged a finger at him. "You don't play fair."

"Not when it comes to something I want." He glanced at Vivi and her mother. "I didn't realize the photographers would be following you or I'd have set up security. Did Owen?"

She shook her head. "It hasn't been that bad."

He frowned, obviously disagreeing. She fully expected him to rip into her agent later today.

"Well, you two, I have some calls to make," Anne Marie said in a light tone. "I'm not working this week but there are a few cases I have to handle." As she smiled at Vivi, her mother's stare lingered, as if to say *behave* before she left the room.

✧   ✧   ✧

SHOWING UP ON Anne Marie Zane's doorstep and offering his condolences for the death of her son was one of the hardest things Landon had ever done. Finding he had to drive past paparazzi pissed him the hell off. He should have been here for her in more ways than one.

He wasn't proud of the fact that he'd bailed on Vivi when she needed him, but he'd been so unsettled by the situation, uncertain whether staying away was better than being by her side when he couldn't feel her pain. Not in the way she probably needed him to. Looking back, he'd taken the coward's way out. He'd steered clear, avoiding her altogether.

She sat at the table wearing a pair of plaid pajama pants and a tank top, the outline of her breasts visible from across the room, her tight nipples puckering through the ribbed shirt.

Landon cleared his throat. "Mind if I join you?" He gestured to the seat her mother had been in earlier.

"Go ahead." Ignoring him, she took another spoonful of what looked like soggy cereal. She swallowed, grimaced, and pushed the bowl out of reach.

And still, she said nothing.

Not that he blamed her. He'd shown up here. Now he had to fumble through whatever he'd come to say.

"I'm sorry."

She lifted her head at that. "For?"

He raised and dropped his shoulders, knowing there was a laundry list of his sins. "Disappearing. Not being there when you needed me. Putting my past hurt before your present pain. You name it, I'm sorry for it." He ducked his head a bit then looked at her again. "I needed time to get my head on straight, and I regret that it came at your expense."

"Thank you." She drew a deep breath, opening and closing her mouth, clearly trying to pull her thoughts together. "I ... didn't expect you to be sorry my brother was dead, but I did think once the shock wore off you'd be there for me ... and you weren't." The words came out in an emotionless tone, the complete opposite of the storm he assumed was brewing inside her.

Guilt swamped him and he reached across the table for her hand, pulling it toward him, keeping his fingers curled around her fist. He needed to touch her, to find a way to break through the wall she'd erected to keep him out.

"I should have been here. No matter who it was who died, someone who mattered to you was gone, you were hurting, and I should have been there for you." Instead he'd holed up in his apartment, remembering the details of the night Levi had died.

The way his brother's drunk body had sagged when Vic had put the backpack full of rocks on his shoulders and insisted he run up and down the stairs. The sound of Levi's head hitting the stairs when he fell backwards, the weight dragging him down. Him screaming for his brother to wake up.

He shook his head, forcing himself away from the old memories.

"Where were you just now?" she asked. "Where did you disappear to?"

He wasn't surprised at how perceptive she was, but he refused to put that night in her head. Before choosing to come find her, he'd decided his future had to come before his past. Vivi had to come first. Because Levi would have wanted Landon to live his life and be happy. And he'd have liked Vivi a lot.

"Nowhere that matters *now*." He peeled open her hand and ran his fingers over her palm. "I should have been there for you and I'm sorry. I promise you it won't happen again. I won't bail on you when you need me ever again."

As she met his gaze, her face free of makeup, her eyes damp, he took in her emotionless expression and something froze inside him.

"I accept your apology. But I think you now know what I meant when I said things between us were too complicated to work."

"But–"

She shook her head. "I have two weekends left at Club TEN29 and a meeting with Owen in a couple of days to decide my immediate future. The one thing I know for certain is that it doesn't involve me staying in New York."

Panic raced through him at her definitive tone, as if she'd made up her mind and what he wanted didn't matter. "And you've never heard of long-distance relationships? We can make it work, Vivi. If you want us badly enough."

She turned a scary glare on him. "Are your parents okay with you being in a relationship with the woman whose brother killed their son?" she asked, dropping the one bomb he'd yet to deal with.

But only because they'd been too busy processing the fact that Vic was dead. He hadn't known how to push them to accept Vivi in that same moment or risk losing their only other son.

"They will come around," he told her with more assurance than he felt. His mother would because she was a romantic at heart. He couldn't swear his father would do the same.

She narrowed her gaze. "You mean they know about me and they don't approve."

Shit, he thought with a wince. He'd forgotten that he hadn't told her that he'd already filled in his parents about their relationship.

"Not a shock," she muttered under her breath. Tears filled her eyes as she said, "I don't even blame them, Landon. I'm a living, breathing reminder of what they lost and how." She jerked her hand out of his and took her bowl to the sink, rinsing it out, her back to him.

He had spent the last couple of days without her and he knew for sure now. She was his. If his parents wanted him in their lives, they had to accept Vivi, too. But telling his parents where he stood would be easier than convincing Vivi to give him another chance.

He rose and strode up behind her, wrapping his arms around her waist, his heart beating a rapid tattoo in his chest. She stiffened at first, then released her tension, letting him hold her.

He leaned his chin on her shoulder and inhaled her warm scent. *I'm going to fix things*, he silently promised. *One way or another, she's going to be mine.*

❖   ❖   ❖

VIVI SAT A car hired by Owen on her way to his office, Ellie by her side. Not only was Ellie her assistant, she was her rock and the only person she wanted with her when Owen laid out her options. Not the only person, a little voice in her head told her, but Vivi ruthlessly pushed it aside. She'd worked hard for this moment and she had to focus on her career, the one sure thing in her life.

Although Landon had made promises in her mother's kitchen, he'd been strangely quiet in the two days since. Oh, she'd received flowers after returning home, treats from Faith's, a new bodyguard suddenly appeared, and Landon had watched her approvingly during rehearsals, a warm glint in his eye.

But he hadn't approached her about having spoken to his parents, and she could only assume either he'd decided not to burden them or they'd stood their ground and he couldn't hurt the couple again by walking out of their lives. Not that she'd want him to do that to them anyway. Screwed up, as she'd always thought.

"We're here!" Ellie's voice broke into Vivi's unpleasant thoughts.

They exited the car. She drew a deep breath and pulled herself together. *Don't accept immediately. Say you'll think about it. Review the contract before signing.* Her mother's wise advice echoed in her head.

Squeezing Ellie's hand once for luck before releasing her friend, Vivi pulled back her shoulders and walked into Owen's office, not surprised to see Axel there along with her agent.

He was wearing a tapered European suit in a bold blue color, which made his white-blond hair even more striking. "Vivi!" He stepped forward and embraced her, causing her to stiffen, but before she could back away, Axel released her. "Business only. I've been warned."

A glance over his shoulder showed her Owen grinning. He'd learned from Landon ... a name she refused to focus on now.

"Vivi, Ellie, Let's sit. Axel has exciting news," Owen said, a gleam in his eye.

Her palms began to sweat as she prepared herself for all sorts of possibilities. Opening for acts on the road or for Vegas residencies. Touring as backup in Europe as many singers did. Any of those things would be a windfall to a starting artist.

"So we'd like to offer you your own tour..." Axel said, and Vivi realized he'd begun speaking. Shit. She was so nervous, thank God she had Ellie here as a second set of ears.

"Vivienne, are you listening? Axel just offered you your own tour!"

"Vivi!" Ellie exclaimed.

"Wait, *what*? You mean opening for someone, right? Who is it?" She rattled off a list of current pop names, certain she hadn't heard him say she was headlining.

"Vivi, I said your *own tour*." Axel was grinning from ear to ear.

"But ... why me?" This wasn't how new singers typically started.

"Clearly you haven't been listening or you're seriously underestimating your sudden rise to fame this summer," Axel said. "One million Instagram followers, Vivi. Add to that your YouTube views and the scalping going on for tickets at Club TEN29? You're a star, baby. Now let me launch you into the stratosphere."

She blinked in utter shock while Ellie's fingernails dug into her arm in excitement. Her friend knew better than to squeal the way she wanted to. The way Vivi wanted to.

"Vivienne?" Owen looked at her with a worried expression.

She ran her tongue over her dry lips and tried to speak past the lack of saliva in her mouth. No matter how excited she was, and she did want to jump up and dance and scream, she understood this was a business deal and she would only have one first opportunity to get it right.

"Draw up the contracts and send them over." She pulled in deep breaths. "I'll be hiring an entertainment lawyer to look things over." Catching Owen about to argue, she shook her head. "I want, I need a second look."

"Fine, fine. Do you want me to recommend someone?" he asked.

She shook her head. "I'll handle it." She needed someone who had her best interests in mind, not her agent's.

She could barely process what was happening around her as Axel rose to his feet. "We're going to do right by you. The music you're recording now will find a home with the perfect label. Your tour will break records, I just know it, and my gut is never wrong."

Everything she'd ever hoped for and dreamed of was coming true, all because she'd taken a trip to a bar one night, needing to sing. Her best friend was by her side. Her mother would be thrilled. So why was there an emptiness in her chest she couldn't relieve?

She rose to her feet and shook Axel's hand, then Owen grasped her palm. "I believed in you from day one, Vivienne. This is just the beginning."

She managed a nod and a smile because she was still in shock.

The next thing she knew, she and Ellie were back on the street, and her best friend shrieked and pulled her into a hug. "Vivi Z. You are going to be a star!" Another scream came after that, and Vivi laughed, finally letting herself feel the energy and excitement that came with accepting this was real. "But why am I sensing sadness, too?" Ellie asked.

"Because you know me well." Vivi sighed. "Landon came to see me at my mother's house the other day."

Ellie's eyes opened wide. "Why didn't you say anything?"

"Because despite the fact that he apologized, key things haven't changed. His parents don't approve, and though normally I'd say fuck it, he's a grown man, we both know why their opinion matters. Imagine them losing another son because of me? Vic's sister?" She shook her head.

A car honked in the street, and another driver got angry and honked longer and louder.

She waited until the pissing contest ended and then started talking again. "I won't be responsible for destroying that family. They've been through enough. So I need to get over Landon Bennett." The words hurt to say and even worse to feel. "Besides, I'm leaving and I'll be traveling all over the world. Even if we worked things out, when would I see him?"

"The family part I understand. The travel? Pfft." Ellie waved a hand through the air. "That's a bullshit excuse and you know it. You're just scared."

She drew in a breath of steamy summer air. "I am not... Yes, I am. I'm petrified," she admitted out loud for the first time. "That man holds my heart in his hands, and if I keep saying it can't work, that it never could work, I'm protecting myself."

"Except you're not. Because you're hurting anyway."

"I am." She looked up into the bright sun and blinked, letting the tears fall. "I love him, Ellie. And I am so scared of losing him I'm not giving him a chance."

Ellie squeezed her hand. "Listen to me. You fell for the one guy that isn't easy. You're both going to have to work at it to have a relationship. The question is, is it worth fighting for?"

Vivi didn't hesitate, nodding immediately. "God, yes. None of this feels as exciting as it could if he was in my life." And he wanted to be there. She was the one pushing him away.

Suddenly she knew what she had to do. The very thought made her want to vomit, but like Ellie said, she had to fight for the life she desired. "I have to go somewhere. Can you catch a cab or an Uber back home?"

Ellie nodded. "Go get your man."

That wasn't exactly what Vivi had in mind. There was something else she needed to handle first.

LANDON SAT ON his parents' back patio, the sun beating down overhead, both his mom and dad staring at him from the double porch swing while Landon sat on a chair across from them. Silence sounded as loud as any band could have considering the bomb he'd dropped not long after arriving.

"Mom, Dad, I love you both. I know you lost Levi, and I don't want to cause you any more pain, but I love Vivi and I'm going to be with her. If you want me to be part of your lives, holidays, birthdays, Sunday dinners, you're going to have to come to terms with our relationship."

His mother blinked back tears, but Landon saw the understanding in her expression. His father? Not so much.

"Do you realize that she's grieving?" Landon asked them. "She didn't like her brother. She didn't have a relationship with him as adults, but she lost a sibling just like I did. And guess what? I left her alone after it happened. I didn't even take her to the car to go see her mother. I just stood there while she walked out."

"Landon!" His mother sounded horrified.

Good. Because he hadn't forgiven himself for that yet. "Don't you see? She's not her brother. I want you to get to know her and judge her for who she is. Not who she's related to."

His mother nodded slowly. "I … I can do that. Because I love you, Landon, and I just want you to be happy. And part of my life." She turned to her husband. "Samuel?"

His father, who had always been a kind, understanding man, rose and folded his arms across his chest, the years of pain, of loss etched in the lines on his face.

Suddenly the doorbell rang, the chimes sounding outside, where they'd installed them so they'd hear if someone came by when they were out by the pool.

"Are you expecting anyone?" his father asked.

His mother shook her head.

"I'll get it," he muttered, taking the excuse to walk out without answering or dealing with the question at hand.

With a sigh, she looked at Landon. "He'll come around. You just have to understand how difficult this all is."

"I do, Mom. Trust me. And so does Vivi. She's the one who doesn't want us to be together because it hurts both of you. She's a good person."

When his father didn't return right away, Landon glanced inside. "Who could it be? If it was a delivery, he'd have been back out here by now."

"Come. Let's go inside and see. I'll talk to him for you, honey."

He wrapped his arm around his mother's shoulder and kissed her cheek. "Thanks. Love you, Mom."

"I love you, too, sweetheart."

Together they headed inside only to find Landon's father standing with Vivi in the entryway of the house.

Landon's heart slammed inside his chest as he took in his father's hard expression and Vivi's pale face.

"Vivi?" Landon strode over and met her gaze. "What are you doing here?"

She gave him a tremulous smile. "I thought it would be a good idea if I talked to your parents." She bit down on her lower lip, obviously nervous.

Too bad that little gesture had him wanting to nibble on the fleshy pout, too.

"Hello, Vivi. I think new introductions are in order, yes? I'm Carrie and you're welcome in my home." His mother put out a hand and touched Vivi's.

Landon let out a relieved sigh but he wasn't truly breathing. Not until his father came around.

"Samuel?" Carrie nudged him with her elbow but Vivi shook her head.

"Please don't force him. I just came today to tell you that I'm very sorry for what my brother did to your son." She drew a heavy sigh. "Vic was a very disturbed boy and man. I didn't have a relationship with him. Neither did my mother. He was just too far gone to help, and my mother couldn't live with the things he'd done."

Vivi's trembling voice put a stranglehold on Landon's heart.

"I realize that I'm a reminder of everything," she went on. "But I want you to know..." Her gaze fell on

Landon. "I love your son. I love him enough to walk away so you don't lose another child by forcing him to give you an ultimatum."

Her words shocked Landon, taking him completely off guard. But her soft gaze never left his as she spoke.

Before he could walk over and pull her into his arms, his father said, "If you're so willing to walk away to give us peace, why are you even here? Why not just let Landon go?" Samuel asked. He sounded genuinely curious, not angry.

Carrie gasped at the question and Landon took a step toward his father, no plan in mind, but Vivi grabbed his arm.

"I came because I wanted to tell you I was sorry. And to explain that I really do love Landon. Whatever you decide, I understand. But if you can find it in your heart to accept me, I'll do everything I can to make him happy." She turned and walked out, leaving them all stunned.

Landon had every intention of following her out, his father's feelings be damned, but he paused to glare at the parent who'd raised him to be a better man. "How could you—"

Samuel shook his head. "Go after her, son," he said in an understanding voice. "I'll be here when you come back. With Vivi. I just wanted to know where her head was. I want the best for you."

With a half nod, Landon turned and ran for the front door, wanting to get to Vivi before a car arrived to take her back to the city.

✦   ✦   ✦

SEVEN MINUTES UNTIL the Uber showed up. Dammit. Vivi glanced at the house and turned away, not wanting anyone to see the tears streaming down her face.

She'd done what she came to do. She'd faced Landon's parents and apologized for her brother and admitted her feelings, although she hadn't anticipated Landon being there when she did. Talk about mortifying. But tomorrow, she'd be able to look in the mirror and know she'd done what she could to salvage a relationship that meant everything to her.

"Vivi!" The door to the house slammed open and Landon strode out, a determined look on his face.

She wrapped her arms around herself and turned to him. "I hope I didn't make things worse with your family. Your father especially."

He shook his head, cupping his hands around her cheeks. "You're one brave woman, Vivi Zane. And I love you, too."

She blinked, forcing the tears to continue to fall. "I'm sorry your father can't accept me but I do understand. I just needed to come and explain my side. I wanted them to see *me*."

He shook his head and smiled. "You did what I couldn't. I gave them an ultimatum, though my mother didn't need one. My father was going to stand his ground, and I was ready to walk away. To come to you regardless of what they wanted. And then you showed up and you softened him." Reaching up, he threaded his fingers through her hair. "I love you, Vivi."

Her heart swelled with love for this man who was willing to choose her. "Really?"

He nodded. "Definitely," he said with a grin. "You know, when I lost my twin, I lost a part of myself. I never thought I'd find anyone who'd complete me. I watched Jason then Tanner pair off, and still, it didn't feel possible for me. Even knowing my parents had a solid thirty-year marriage, I thought I'd be alone. And then I met you and something about you called to me."

She slid her hands around his waist. "I felt it, too. At first I chalked it up to just attraction, but there was a deeper pull. I've never been in love before either. But I love you. Enough to put your family's happiness above my own."

"Listen to me, Vivienne Zane. *You* are *my* happiness. And we're stronger together. So from now on, we're a team."

"A long-distance team?" she asked.

He narrowed his gaze. "Did you get news from Owen?"

She held her breath before telling him, knowing this meant they'd be pulled apart just when they'd gotten together. Would he share in her excitement and joy? Or would the reality make him sorry he'd chosen her?

"Vivi? Tell me." His hands slid from her cheeks to her forearms.

"Axel – who was on his best behavior thanks to you talking to Owen – offered me my own world tour."

A few silent beats passed while he processed the news. "Holy shit, Vivi."

She nodded. "My thoughts exactly." She pulled her lower lip between her teeth.

Before she could ask him his feelings, he picked her up and swung her around. "That's my girl! You're going places and I'm so fucking proud of you!"

He spun her twice until she was dizzy and laughing out loud. "Put me down!" Although he complied, he held on to her, his hands around her waist as he pulled her against him.

"I can't wait to see you conquer the world," he said, warmth and honest pride in his eyes.

God, this man. He was so special and good to her. Good *for* her. "What about us?"

"I'm not going anywhere. We'll make it work." And with that pronouncement, he bent his head and captured her lips with his.

Once his mouth met hers, all the longing and desire she'd kept tucked away came roaring back with a vengeance. His tongue curled around hers as he kissed her in front of the entire neighborhood and she didn't care.

Not when the man she loved had her in his arms. She still didn't know how they'd handle a long-distance future, but she was going to do everything she could to make sure they stayed together.

Forever.

Epilogue

VIVI ENDED HER last song at Club TEN29, though she'd already been informed she had an open invitation to return any time. She performed an encore, a new song she'd been working on recording in the studio. The experience felt so different now, knowing she'd be performing her music across the world.

The good news was the album would come first, no travel until she completed her music, so she and Landon had more time together in New York and she'd have more time with her mom, who was still grieving Vic's death. She was about to walk offstage to the audience clapping when Landon unexpectedly joined her.

"How about another round of applause for our summer star!" he said, raising their now joined hands in the air.

She took her bows and met Landon's gaze, shocked by the emotion she saw in his expression and the love gleaming from his eyes. Not that she didn't know how he felt—he showed her every night—but this was a public expression of his feelings.

He held on to her hand, turning it over so her palm faced down. She sensed the moment the audience felt the change in him … in them, and a hush fell over the club as he slipped his free hand into his pants pocket.

"Landon?"

He removed his hand, cupping something in his fist. "Vivi?" Taking her completely off guard, he dropped down on one knee.

Her heart lodged in her throat.

"I know it's soon but when you know, you know. And I am certain I don't want to spend another minute without you by my side." The sensitive microphone on stage picked up his words and a murmur of *awws*, filled the air. "I also know that I don't want to be apart when you take off to fulfill your dreams. So."

Eyes opened wide, tears brimming, she listened, happiness filling her with everything he said.

"I'm going with you on tour. You need someone besides Ellie who has your back, and the guys can handle the club while I travel. I'll come back every so often to check and make sure they aren't running this place into the ground, of course."

"But your life…"

"Is with you. I'll be your business manager. Your

bodyguard. Your lover and your best friend. So, Vivi, will you marry me?"

"Say yes!" a familiar voice called from the back of the room. Tanner, she thought.

She blinked and tears fell as she nodded. "Yes."

He slipped the ring onto her finger, and a chorus of applause broke out around them.

He stood and pulled her into his arms. "The business manager thing was a joke," he said, whispering for her ears alone. "I'll be anything you need me to be as long as we can be together."

Looping her arms around his neck, she grinned. "I need a team around me I can trust. We will find an official role for you because there is no one I trust more. I love you, Landon Bennett."

His lips brushed hers. "And I love you, Vivi Zane soon to be Bennett. Now come on. I have a surprise in the dressing room."

He led her off the stage and into the back room. Inside, everyone she knew was there. Tanner and Scarlett, Jason and Faith, her mom, who was crying and beaming at the same time, Ellie with her big, happy grin, Amber and her son, and even Owen had made an appearance.

But when she turned toward her dressing table, the biggest surprise awaited. Landon's parents stood to the side. Holding her hand, Landon walked toward them.

Samuel and Carrie met them halfway. "Welcome to the family," Landon's father, the last one to have come around to accept her, said, warmth in his tone. "I always wanted a daughter."

She swallowed the lump in her throat. "But I... You..."

"Let's go on from here, okay?" Samuel reached out and held her hand in his. "You make my son happy and that's all I care about now."

"I promise to always put him first. I can't believe he's going on tour with me."

"You couldn't keep me away." Landon ran a hand down the back of her hair. "We're a team."

She grinned at his parents. "I think he learned that from the two of you."

After sharing a glass of champagne and enjoying toasts, Landon excused them and dragged her upstairs. She was glad he hadn't thrown her over his shoulder in front of friends and family, but she was grateful to finally be alone.

She looked down at the crazy glitzy ring he'd bought her and sighed with pleasure. "I wouldn't have thought I was a girl who loved bling, but this ring is gorgeous."

"When you're out there performing for the world, I just want everyone to know you're mine."

She lifted herself to her toes and pressed a warm

kiss on his lips. "Yours and only yours. Forever."

❖   ❖   ❖

THE DOUBLE WEDDING of Tanner and Scarlett and Landon and Vivi took place the weekend before Vivi was due to leave on tour. Knowing the dates ahead of time, Vivi and Landon had snuck off to Tahiti for a pre-wedding honeymoon alone, then returned in time to get married. The venue was Club TEN29, where, they all agreed, Levi's presence would be felt the most.

When Vivi walked down the aisle to Landon, her mother on one side, his father on the other because she had no one else to give her away, she literally took his breath away.

Her hair fell in a tumble of dark waves around her shoulders, the shawl-like top of the dress draping around her forearms, her face shimmering with excitement and love. Love Landon reciprocated tenfold.

"Breathe," Tanner muttered, much as Landon had said to him a few minutes ago when Scarlett had made her way toward him on her father's arm. Her mother was still in the assisted living facility, where she was nonverbal and nonresponsive. But today was about celebrating.

As Scarlett faced Tanner and Vivi looked to Landon, holding hands, they said their vows, promising to

219

love, honor, and cherish, in sickness and in health. Landon barely heard the words.

All he cared about was making Vivi his. And after he kissed the bride, dipping her low and covering her lips with his, he did just that, joining them together for the rest of their lives.

Considering the obstacles they'd had to overcome, he was pretty damned happy and satisfied as they strode back down the aisle, following Tanner and Scarlett out.

Next week they had a concert tour to begin. Tonight he'd make Vivi his in every way that mattered.

WHAT'S NEXT?

The DARES are back with hot new heroes and stories:

Order DARE TO RESIST out soon!

Read Dare to Resist Chapter One!

Dare to Resist

Dare Nation Novel #1

Chapter One

Q UINNLYN STONE SASHAYED out of Austin Prescott's office, sweet curves encased in a tight black skirt with high fuck me heels completing the outfit.

"Stop staring at your assistant's ass or at the very least don't be obvious about it."

Austin Prescott, sport agent to the stars, co-head of Dare Nation Sports Management, cupped the back of his neck in his hand and let out a groan.

"You're right," he said to Marcus Powers, an agent in his office and a close friend. "It's not cool." Quinn was the best executive assistant ever and Austin didn't want to lose her.

She was extremely intelligent, could keep up with negotiations, handle the wise-ass players Austin represented, and on the times they went out for meals, make small talk with their fancy wives. Oh and she tasted like the sweetest treat he'd ever had.

He knew because they'd had one slip. He'd been a week post surgical procedure and she'd come to visit, bringing work with her. She'd reached for papers, her hand brushed his dick and nature had taken its course. He hadn't been able to shift his body but their eyes met, giving her plenty of time to say no. Hell, knowing how badly he wanted her, he'd even told her she ought to move away. She'd remained and his mouth had sealed over hers and fireworks erupted. Though they'd both agreed it was a mistake and they'd never brought it up again, he hadn't been able to forget.

Quinn was a different sort of woman than the groupies who used to chase him in his NFL days. Everything about her appealed to him but he did his best to treat her with the utmost respect. When he wasn't inadvertently staring at her ass, that is. It was dicey to have an affair with a co-worker, someone for whom he was directly in charge of her career. And she didn't strike him as a one and done kind of woman and that was his M.O. Not that he thought one time with Quinn would be enough.

"Are you going to Allstars tonight?" Marcus asked of the exclusive sports and cigar bar in South Beach that catered to the elite athlete.

It was a place players and industry people could

frequent without groupies and hangers on bothering them. Which wasn't to say Austin couldn't find a woman to hook up with there. Just that there was a higher class of female to choose from than a run of the mill establishment.

He ran a hand over his face. Maybe hanging out with friends and possibly going home with a woman was just what he needed to take the edge off this gnawing desire for Quinn. Since he'd put his rampant playboy days behind him, he was more discriminating and discreet, yet it had still been too long since he'd gotten laid.

"Sure. I'll be there."

"Awesome." Marcus pulled out his phone to check his email.

Just then, Austin's desk phone buzzed and he picked up the receiver. "Yes?"

"You're needed in the conference room. You and Marcus both," Quinn said in her normal voice. But he even found her husky tone arousing. "Can I let your sister know you're coming?" she asked.

"Tell her we'll be right there."

His sister was Dare Nation's publicist and although she wasn't a full partner, she had a definite say in how things ran around here. Brianne was the firm and family *fixer* as they affectionately called her. If something went wrong, she sorted out the issue. A fight between brothers and there were five Prescott siblings in total, spanning nine years? She put herself in the middle. She definitely provided a referee between them.

"We're wanted in the conference room. Apparently Bri's called a meeting." Austin pushed up from his chair.

"Any idea what she wants?" Marcus asked.

He shook his head. "Not a clue but we might as well go find out."

He headed for the conference room, Marcus right behind him, stepped inside and heard, "Surprise!"

Blinking into the bright room, he realized the entire staff was present, along with his family. In the corners, gold and white balloons decorated the room and a large cake sat on the rectangular gleaming wood table.

"What is all this?" he asked, confused. It wasn't his birthday.

Bri sidled up beside him, her long blonde hair pulled into a bun at the back of her head. "Today is one year since the kidney transplant. A year since you saved Uncle Paul's life."

Paul Dare walked up to him, looking healthy, his skin tanned, his eyes clear and gleaming. "Thank you ... son."

Everyone in this room knew the word son meant

so much more to both than a random term of endearment. Uncle was the name they'd given the man who'd been close to the family growing up. *Son* was still their new reality.

Paul Dare was the Prescott siblings' biological father, something that had been revealed when Paul needed a kidney transplant last year. When Jesse Prescott, the man who'd raised them as his own, hadn't been able to have children, Austin's mother, Christine, had turned to her best friend since childhood to help her via sperm donation. Her gay best friend. The man she'd been in love with but couldn't have. To say it had been a shock was an understatement.

"You're welcome," Austin said to Paul, who he still called *uncle*. Despite Jesse's harsh parenting skills, he'd raised Austin and deserved respect. But Jesse had died when Austin was twenty-one, and there was no doubt that his absence made the discovery of his biological father easier to handle.

When Paul came to them with his need for a kidney, all the siblings had been tested to be donors. Austin had been the exact match and never once thought of denying the man who'd been more of a kind presence in their lives than their own father had been. His brothers and sister each had their own reaction to the news that Paul was their biological dad but since they all agreed Jesse had been a tough bastard and *Uncle* Paul had been there for them, the adjustment hadn't been a bad one.

Austin pulled the older man into a brief hug before releasing him. "Any chance you and Ron will come to Allstars tonight? Marcus and I are going."

"I'll be there," Bri chimed in.

"We'll try. Ron's been sick this week. I'll see if he's feeling up to it," Paul said of his long-time partner, Ron Mayburn. Another Prescott family friend who'd been loyal to them for years.

"Give him my best and don't push him if he's not up to it. And let's do dinner soon. The three of us," Austin said.

"Sounds good." Paul smiled. "So what about you? When are you going to settle down?"

Austin grimaced at the thought. "I like my life the way it is, thank you very much."

"Really? You like going home alone at night to a house that echoes because it's so big but empty? Ordering in dinner? Eating by yourself?" Paul lowered his voice so they wouldn't be overheard.

"Whoah, what is with the third degree?" Austin asked, surprised.

"I just worry about all of you. Single. Alone. Even your mother seems open to a new relationship but you kids?" He shook his head. "I just want the best for you."

One look into his serious indigo eyes and Austin knew they were related. It was a miracle none of them had caught on sooner but then no one ever had a reason to assume they weren't Jesse Prescott's children by blood.

"Well trust me, I'm not always lonely." Austin winked at his uncle, unwilling to admit that just maybe the truth hit a little close to home. But not enough to consider settling down any time soon. If anything, he was now even more determined to get laid and get rid of this annoying desire for someone he couldn't admit to clawing at him inside.

"I'm always here if you need me," Paul said before turning to talk to one of the agents in the office.

Letting out a breath, Austin took a minute to just *be*, before he made the rounds as well, thanking everyone for showing up for this impromptu party.

Before he could begin, Quinn came up to him, a warm smile on her beautiful face. "I know I've said it before but you did a wonderful thing for Paul and for your family," she said, her green eyes shining with admiration.

Her approval meant something to him he couldn't quite name but her praise also made him uncomfortable. "I just did what anyone would do." He shifted on his feet.

She shook her head, a wry smile lifting her lips. "That's what makes what you did so special. You really believe it was no big deal." She reached up and patted his cheek, obviously meaning it to be a friendly tap but their eyes met and her touch lingered.

With her soft hand against his face, he wanted nothing more than to grab her wrist, pull her close and kiss her … again. Since the yearning had been building for a year, and knowing he was no longer incapacitated by surgery, their union wouldn't be soft and sweet, either.

A loud laugh broke the silence. Cheeks flushed, Quinn stepped back and turned away, walked to the table and began cutting the cake, head down, not meeting his gaze.

Not well done of him, he thought and groaned. Time to focus on the gathering around him and his workers. He clapped his hands. "Okay everyone, eat cake, be merry, and head home for the day. My way of showing my appreciation for the party."

That pronouncement earned him a round of applause. Even if it was already four p.m. on a Friday, leaving early was leaving early and cutting his employees some slack was good for morale.

He waited until he'd spoken to and thanked everyone, and made certain he was the last to leave the office before heading out, locking up behind him.

Then Austin, Bri and Marcus met up for a steak dinner. Afterwards they settled in at Allstars for a drink and well deserved relaxation. The dark oak walls of the bar, the low sconce lighting and the comfortable club chairs settled him.

"Hello, Austin, long time no see." Marnie, a cocktail waitress at the bar, sidled up close to him.

"Hi, yourself. How are you?" he asked.

She batted her lashes. "How do I look?" she asked flirtatiously.

He chuckled at the way she deliberately was fishing for compliments. They had history, he and Marnie, as in he'd fallen into bed with her once before.

With her auburn hair that hung long and wavy around her shoulders and a killer body, she was easy on the eyes. She didn't do it for him like a certain green-eyed assistant but *she* was off limits. Marnie wasn't.

He dragged his gaze up her long legs in black pants up to her silk camisole, also black. Her breasts were perky and her smile welcoming. "You look pretty damn fine from where I'm sitting," he said.

Marnie grinned, gripping her round cocktail tray in her hands. "So what can I get for you?" she asked in a husky voice.

"The usual." A Don Julio would sit well right now.

"And maybe a little something later? My shift ends

early tonight," she offered, leaning down so he could see her lush cleavage.

Austin grinned because he'd just found his willing woman to take home for the night.

✧　✧　✧

QUINNLYN STONE WALKED into Allstars with her brother, Matt, by her side. Although she'd wanted nothing more than to go home after work, he'd insisted they needed to meet and talk in person. Worried about him because she was the oldest of four siblings and that had always been her job to watch out for the others, she'd agreed but insisted on going someplace quiet. After the party at the office and being around people for an hour in a small room, she wanted some peace.

These days, crowds and loud noises made her a little anxious. She likened it to a mild form of PTSD, similar to her cousin who had had an extremely colicky baby. Even a decade later, she couldn't listen to an infant crying without being transported back to the intense feelings of failure and frustration of those days.

Growing up, Quinn felt like she'd run a daycare. Her parents even thought, given her experience, she should become a nanny, but Quinn had put herself through college and business school on scholarship and loans instead. And that's why she loved her job.

She worked for one man, it was often quiet, and she was doing something for herself for a change.

Allstars was on the top level of an exclusive hotel, but she waited in the lobby for her brother because it was hot and humid in Miami in August. She hadn't seen her brother in a while because he'd missed last month's Sunday dinner at her parent's house.

When he walked in, she grinned. "Matty!" She ran up and wrapped her arms around him, hugging him tight before releasing him and taking him in. His jet black hair was combed, his glasses with black frames sat on his face, and his sport jacket was perfectly pressed. "Look at my baby brother in his college professor attire."

He chuckled but rolled his eyes. "You're twenty-eight. I'm two years younger than you. Jeffrey's the baby."

At twenty-one, yes he was. But so was Matt. "As long as you're younger, you're the baby, so humor me."

"I am humoring you. I'm letting you bring me to a place where jocks hang out, aren't I?"

She wrinkled her nose. "That's a snobby, elitist thing to say. Now, come. Let's go have a drink and you can tell me why you wanted to see me." She clasped his hand, led him to the elevator and hit the button for the top floor.

They walked out and as they waited for the hostess to lead them to a table, she heard a familiar laugh that sent tingles down her spine and a jolt of pure awareness through her veins. After hearing his voice all day, she should be immune to such a typical feminine reaction. Quinn always knew when Austin Prescott was nearby.

"Your table is ready," an attractive waitress with blonde highlights in her hair, said.

"Thank you." They started for the table when Quinn heard her name. "We'll be right there," she said to the other woman.

"Matt, come say hello to Austin."

"The jock boss," he said low enough for her to hear.

"What do you have against athletes?" she asked. The rest of the family loved sports. She came by her choice of job naturally. Her dad was a die-hard Miami Thunder fan.

"I know their social reputations. I just don't want you to end up a notch in this guy's bedpost."

Her eyes opened wide. "Oh my God, Matt! He's been nothing but professional since I started working for him." If she ignored the one kiss that consumed her dreams.

She pulled her brother over to Austin's table, where he sat with Bri and Marcus. "Matt, you've met

Austin. This is his sister, Bri who works PR at the firm and Marcus who is an agent. Guys, this is my brother, Matt."

They all exchanged hellos.

"I didn't know you'd be here tonight," she said to Austin, who looked casual and relaxed. His white shirt was unbuttoned, showing a smattering of chest hair she had to drag her eyes away from. And right now those gorgeous unique colored indigo eyes were hot on her face.

"I was dragged here by these two." He gestured to the others at the table. "What brings you out tonight?"

She glanced at her sibling. "Matt wanted to talk. I figured this place was a good choice."

Austin inclined his head. "So I don't suppose I can convince you to join us?"

She smiled but shook her head. "I need to know what Matt wants."

A low laugh sounded from beside her. "I want a drink."

Quinn grinned. "And that's my cue. I'll see you Monday?" she asked.

Austin nodded. "See you Monday."

Matt grasped her hand and led her to the table the hostess had indicated earlier and a little while later, she sat with a glass of Chardonnay, while her brother drank a scotch and soda. They talked about home, their parents, their siblings and their jobs, catching up. But all the while, she was acutely aware of Austin. And the waitress who was definitely flirting with him in ways that couldn't be misconstrued.

Quinn ought to be used to the attention Austin garnered. From the first business lunch they'd attended, women ignored Quinn and threw themselves at Austin. He had cleavage lowered into in his face, boobs brushed against his arm, phone numbers slipped into his jacket pocket ... and she could go on. He laughed it off to being an ex-NFL star.

But she'd Googled him prior to her interview for the job in order to gain information about the man. What she'd learned besides his stats – the fact that he was a Heisman Trophy winner and Rookie of the Year for the Thunder as quarterback – was his reputation with women. Though he'd never been linked with one female for long, photos showed him with gorgeous, willowy thin dates on his arm.

Models, actresses, Instagram worthy females who fit his playboy image. He'd been discreet in the time Quinn had been working for him. He'd didn't parade women in the office and never had he asked her to make a lunch or dinner reservation for a date. But the man wasn't a monk and he clearly had no intention of settling down.

"Quinnie-Boo, God are you even listening to me?"

She blinked when Matt snapped his fingers in front of her face and even called her by that awful childhood nickname to get her attention. "I'm sorry. I was lost in thought. But I'm paying attention now." She couldn't spend time thinking about her boss and his strong chiseled features and tanned skin. Or the muscled body beneath the suit. She needed to stop letting her mind wander there.

"I guess you want to know why I asked to see you in person?" Matt asked.

Finally, he got to the crux of things. "I take it you didn't just want to see your sister?"

He shook his head. "I mean of course I did but I also wanted to tell you something." Her brother looked like he was chewing glass, that what he had to reveal was that upsetting.

"What is it?" She put her hand on his.

"I ran into Daniel at a faculty meeting on campus."

She startled at the mention of her ex-fiance. "Oh. Okay?" She and Daniel had ended things on an awkward note.

Matt had introduced them because he and Daniel were colleagues at the smaller college where they both taught. She and Daniel had bonded over the notion that neither one of them wanted children. As the oldest of the family, she'd raised her siblings and was quite content with any nieces or nephews that might

235

come along who she could spoil.

She'd *thought* they'd been on the same page. So when he'd asked her to marry him, it seemed like the right thing to do. They enjoyed each other's company and could each focus on their careers. Until the day he revealed he really did want kids and had assumed she'd change her mind at some point in time.

When she assured him she hadn't … wouldn't … he'd asked her to at least agree to reconsider things down the road. But she knew better than to go into a marriage with something as fundamental as wanting children undecided. She'd ended things and hadn't seen him in two years.

"And?" she asked into the silence.

Matt drummed his fingers against the table. "His wife is pregnant and I wanted you to hear it from me. In case you took it hard or had had second thoughts." He stared at her with love and concern in his eyes and she adored him for it but she did not understand her family.

Her parents thought after helping to raise their kids and her younger cousins she'd want to be a nanny instead of having a career and her brother believed she'd be hurt by her ex doing exactly what he'd told her he'd wanted. Or maybe the problem was her family just didn't understand her.

"I'm fine. Why wouldn't I be? I knew Daniel

wanted kids. Well eventually I knew, although it would have been nice if he'd told me from the beginning and not assumed I'd change my mind."

She glanced at her sibling who still looked worried. "I realized pretty quickly after we broke up that I didn't love him the way I should or I would have been a lot more upset by the end of things." She bit down on her lower lip, remembering that odd feeling of relief after things had ended.

"And by the way, same goes for him. He was engaged again within a year. It's all good, Matt, but thank you for worrying about me." She squeezed her brother's hand and he let out a relieved breath.

From the corner of her eye, she saw the waitress approach Austin once more, lean down and whisper in his ear. Whatever she said, it was an intimate action that had nothing to do with his drink order and he placed his hand on her waist and squeezed once in reply, causing Quinn's stomach to twist at the sight.

"Well I'm glad to hear you're okay," her brother said, oblivious to her inner turmoil over Austin.

She forced a smile still keeping an eye out as Austin reached inside his pants pocket for his wallet, handing the waitress his credit card. She strode off and brought the bill back for him to sign. And not five minutes later, Austin stood up, hugged his sister, shook hands with Marcus and started for the door, meeting up with the woman who'd obviously just gotten off her shift. Together they walked out the door.

But not before Austin turned back and his gaze caught on Quinn's. She hadn't meant to continue staring. Hadn't anticipated him turning back and looking her way. Something flashed in his expression before he shuttered it and quickly jerked his head back around and headed out the door.

Quinn sighed. As much as she hated to admit it, watching Austin with another woman hurt more than breaking up with her ex had. She'd grown close to Austin while working for him and had kept that kiss they'd shared close to her heart.

Until today, she hadn't had to see him with one of his conquests and reality was a bitter pill to swallow. The truth was, she had no business having feelings for her boss. Her job was too good to lose. It allowed her to pay off her student loans and live in an extremely nice, safe apartment complex.

He had every right to do his thing and she'd do her own. Live and let live. And she'd move forward secure in the knowledge her heart wouldn't get broken by her playboy boss.

GET DARE TO RESIST!

Want even more Carly books?
CARLY'S BOOKLIST by Series – visit:
http://smarturl.it/CarlyBooklist

Sign up for Carly's Newsletter:
http://smarturl.it/carlynews

Carly on Facebook:
facebook.com/CarlyPhillipsFanPage

Carly on Instagram:
instagram.com/carlyphillips

About the Author

NY Times, Wall Street Journal, and USA Today Bestseller, Carly Phillips gives her readers Alphalicious heroes to swoon for and romance to set your heart on fire. She married her college sweetheart and lives in Purchase, NY along with her three crazy dogs: two wheaten terriers and a mutant Havanese, who are featured on her Facebook and Instagram. The author of 50 romance novels, she has raised two incredible daughters who put up with having a mom as a full time writer. Carly's book, The Bachelor, was chosen by Kelly Ripa as a romance club pick and was the first romance on a nationally televised bookclub. Carly loves social media and interacting with her readers. Want to keep up with Carly? Sign up for her newsletter (below) and receive TWO FREE books at www.carlyphillips.com.

Made in the USA
Middletown, DE
11 June 2020

97356851R00139

Insta-love only happens in the movies.
Insta-lust? That she'd buy into.
Until she meets take-charge club owner Landon Bennett
and falls head over heels at a glance.

When hot as sin Landon Bennet offers sexy songstress Vivienne Clark a summer residency at his popular Manhattan nightclub, it's the opportunity of a lifetime and she can't resist. Add in the man's obvious interest and seductive attention and life is perfect. Until she puts together the pieces of his past. Fate might have brought them together, but is the intimate relationship they've been building strong enough to overcome the the secret Vivi is hiding?

CARLY ♥ PHILLIPS
New York Times Bestselling Author

CARLYPHILLIPS.COM

ISBN 9781947089358

90000

9 781947 089358